"Whoo hooo, Sable?"

An unadorned female hand with neat trim nails waved in front of her face, bringing her back to the here and now. Her boss was standing right next to her.

"Huh?" Sable stared blankly down at the tiny woman.

Dressed in a business suit with her blonde hair pulled back in a meticulous French twist, Miranda Grey looked out of place. Behind the bar of a neighborhood pub that catered to the blue-collar crowd, she was like a mouse at a catnip convention.

"Oh!" Sable snapped back to the present. "Sorry, Mandy, what was that?"

"You look like you just got hit by a truck. What's up?"

While Sable didn't have many friends, the ones she did have, she trusted implicitly. So she blurted out her feelings without hesitation. "You know how I've never understood it when men I barely know call me Trouble?"

"Yes." A tiny frown furrowed her brow.

"Now I understand why."

Miranda followed her gaze to where the stranger was chalking a cue. "He called you Trouble?"

"No. He is Trouble!"

"Ahhh." Miranda's head cocked to the side and she eyed her curiously. "Why?"

She turned to her friend with a devilish smile.

"Because he makes me wanna be bad."

Gypsy Heart

By Sasha White

A Samhain Publishing, Ltd. publication.

Samhain Publishing, Ltd.
2932 Ross Clark Circle, #384
Dothan, AL 36301

Gypsy Heart
Copyright © 2006 by Sasha White
Cover by Scott Carpenter
Print ISBN: 1-59998-129-7
Digital ISBN: 1-59998-053-3
www.samhainpublishing.com

First Samhain Publishing, Ltd. electronic publication: April 2006
First Samhain Publishing, Ltd. print publication: July 2006
The book has been previously published.

Gypsy Heart

By Sasha White

Dedication

To my mom, who raised me to believe that nothing is impossible if you set your mind to it.

Chapter One

Sable Castle jerked her wrist quickly, sending the bottle of vodka twisting around her hand in a flashy spin before she poured an ounce in the glass waiting on the scarred bar. She set the glass in front of one smiling guy before moving on to the next customer in line. Northern Alberta was in the middle of a summer heat wave and people were flocking to any place with air conditioning. Add to that the fact that it was Friday Happy Hour at The Zodiac, and the pub was hopping.

The hair on the back of her neck stood up sharply and instinct made her glance toward the door at the exact moment *he* stepped through it, entering the noisy pub. Mick Jagger's complaining about not getting any satisfaction faded into the background, along with the dozen or so customers standing directly in front of her vying for her attention at the oak bar.

Wow!

Her mind went blank and her hands stilled as she let her eyes roam over him in appreciation.

He radiated 'bad ass' with rough stubble along his jaw and shaggy midnight hair that brushed against the back of his neck. He had the air of a guy that knew how to show a girl a good time, and did so on a regular basis.

Looking him up and down, she took in the faded jeans and tight black T-shirt that covered a body good enough to eat, or at least nibble on.

Oh Yeah.

She unconsciously licked her lips and brought her gaze up to his face only to find him watching her, a small smile twisting his lips. A fire started in her belly, bringing long dormant needs awake with a roar. Unable to tear her gaze away, she watched as he moved toward the bar, toward her, until the crowd shifted and the spell was broken.

Thank God.

With her cleavage baring tops and tight jeans, Sable might play up the image of the 'bad girl bartender' but it was mostly an act.

She had no problems flirting with customers and talking to anyone about anything under the sun when she was behind the bar. That was her job.

But when a man like that came around, a man that made her heartbeat pick up and her mind slow down, she had to fight not to morph back into that thirteen-year-old that had worn a C-cup when all the other girls were still stuffing their training bras. The one that had learned at an early age that boys, and men, were more interested in what was under her clothes than what was in her head.

A boisterous voice called her name and she glanced at the twenty-something hottie with the gaudy paper hat perched on his head.

"What can I get ya, cutie?" she asked him.

With a flip of her tousled curls and a saucy wink at the Birthday Boy, she forced herself to focus on work. She'd been joking with them for the last half hour or so while they hung out in front of her bar, and took turns ordering drinks and hitting on her.

This new shade of "Rock Star Red" lipstick was doing the trick tonight. The men were lining up and she could see her tip jar getting fuller by the hour. They flirted outrageously, and while none of them made her heart skip a beat, she still enjoyed every minute of it. Not much in life could feed a girl's ego like a line-up of men panting after her.

These boys were out to have a good time and she accepted, even reveled in, the fact that she was part of the entertainment.

"How about a kiss?" the Birthday Boy asked, a silly grin on his face.

"Sure, honey. What the Birthday Boy wants, the Birthday Boy gets," Sable said with a smile as she turned to grab a bottle off the back bar amidst the hoots and hollers his friends let loose.

She slapped a shot glass on the bar, filled it with Cinnamon Schnapps and Baileys before sliding it across the bar to him with a wink.

"Here's a sweet Cinnamon Kiss from me to you."

The group laughed and slapped him on the back as he saluted her with the shot before tossing it back. The ribald comments and laughter made it clear the pub was full of playful men tonight.

Her grin widened. The night was bound to be a challenge, and all she could think was, *bring it on*!

A deep voice interrupted the laughter.

"Whoever said 'Ask and you shall receive' should've told you to be more specific when asking a lady for favors."

"Gage! You made it!" The Birthday Boy cried out in surprise.

"Of course I did. I told you I would, didn't I?"

Sable watched as the men embraced fiercely, their affection for one another obvious. She felt an unusual shyness slip over her at the sexy stranger's appearance and glanced around for a distraction.

Katie, the waitress working the floor, stood at the other end of the bar with an impatient expression on her face, so Sable walked down to that end and filled her order while the group of men greeted the late arrival.

Awareness flowed through her as she heard his deep voice return greetings with natural warmth. She continued to sneak peeks at him as she worked and felt her confidence, and her heart rate, surge when she caught him watching her too.

She knew she was pretty—men hit on her all the time. Mind you...they were usually too young, too old, or too married for her tastes. *Mental note: Check out his left hand!*

Typical of most things in life, the men she liked, the ones that made her think naked thoughts, never hit on her. And since she didn't believe in wasting her time dating someone for the sake of dating, she'd reached the ripe old age of twenty-nine without ever having a 'real' relationship. Not that she was a virgin. She'd had lovers. She'd just never had a boyfriend.

She'd just finished putting Katie's order together when she heard one of the guys in the birthday group suggest they go to the back, where the pool tables were, for an impromptu tournament. Everyone in that group shuffled away amidst a chorus of challenges issued and bets being made.

Everyone except him.

He leaned casually against the bar and watched her move back in his direction.

Grrrrrr. Yum!

The fire in her blood spread, and she fought the old urge to hunch her shoulders and slouch. Instead, she put an extra swing in her hips and pasted a saucy smile on her face. She was not that overdeveloped teenager anymore. She was a woman. One that knew how to use her looks to get what she wanted.

"Hi there," she purred, stopping directly in front of him. Glancing down, she quickly checked out his bare ring finger. "Can I get you something to drink?"

"Bottle of Bud, please." A small smile lifted one corner of his mouth as he let his gaze roam over her body. The appreciation in his eyes made it clear that while some men might like the anorexic model look, he definitely enjoyed the sight of a woman with a bit more to her.

Dressed in a filmy rayon blouse that clung to her full breasts before flowing softly about her trim waist and a pair of tight jeans that stretched to cover her rounded hips, Sable knew she looked sassy, sexy, and all *woman.*

She pulled his beer out of the cooler and turned back in time to catch his gaze on her ass. Exhilaration coursed through her body, making her nipples tighten and her cheeks flush. She welcomed the rush of sensations, and didn't try to hide it.

A smile played at her lips and she quirked an eyebrow at him. "Anything else?"

He looked into her eyes for a long moment before replying. The answering flash of desire in his chocolate eyes made it clear he understood the loaded question.

"Not right now, thanks." He winked, tossed a bill on the bar, grabbed his beer, and walked away.

Sable was glad he didn't look back. Her knees had grown so weak at the reflected heat in his gaze she had to clutch the bar to stay upright.

Whew!

"Whoo hooo, Sable?"

An unadorned female hand with neat trim nails waved in front of her face, bringing her back to the here and now. Her boss was standing right next to her.

"Huh?" Sable stared blankly down at the tiny woman.

Dressed in a business suit with her blonde hair pulled back in a meticulous French twist, Miranda Grey looked out of place. Behind the bar of a neighborhood pub that catered to the blue-collar crowd, she was like a mouse at a catnip convention.

"Oh!" Sable snapped back to the present. "Sorry, Mandy, what was that?"

Miranda was more than just The Zodiac's owner; she was also Sable's best friend. The open expression of amusement on Mandy's face at the moment made Sable think she wasn't hiding her feelings well at all, and Mandy's words confirmed it.

"You look like you just got hit by a truck. What's up?"

While Sable didn't have many friends, the ones she did have, she trusted implicitly. So she blurted out her feelings without hesitation. "You know how I've never understood it when men I barely know call me Trouble?"

"Yes." A tiny frown furrowed her brow.

"Now I understand why."

Miranda followed her gaze to where the stranger was chalking a cue. "He called you Trouble?"

"No. He is Trouble!"

"Ahhh." Miranda's head cocked to the side and she eyed her curiously. "Why?"

She turned to her friend with a devilish smile.

"Because he makes me wanna be bad."

Chapter Two

Gage joined the group at the pool tables. There was no reason for him to stand at the bar and flirt with the enticing bartender. He reminded himself he'd turned over a new leaf. No more casual relationships or party girls, he wanted to find himself a nice girl to settle down with. Besides, he was at the bar to help his little brother celebrate his twenty-fifth birthday, not to hook up with a woman.

"How's it feel to know that you're officially a quarter of a century old, bro?" he asked, slinging his arm around Garret's shoulders.

"Feels pretty damn good to me. Especially since I know that no matter how old I get, you'll always be older, slower, and uglier!"

That got a round of guffaws from the group. With dark hair and dark eyes, neither man had to chase women to get dates, but Garret was definitely the 'pretty boy' version to Gage's rough good looks.

Gage smirked. "At least you recognize the fact that I'll always be smarter."

Garret laughed and choked on the swig of beer he'd just taken, causing Gage to add, "And more graceful."

The jokes stopped for a few minutes while the guys figured out who was playing first. Gage knew most of the men in their group, a combination of Garret's friends from school and his summer job working the rap attack crews.

In fact, he'd trained some of them up in Hinton, a small city smack in the middle of the Rocky Mountains, when they'd first joined the forestry brigade, and he knew they worked hard rappelling out of helicopters into the mountains to fight forest fires. Full of piss and vigor, they played as hard as they worked.

An almost parental pride swelled in his chest when he looked at Garret. The first few years after their father had passed away had been hard on them both, but they'd made it through the toughest of times, and he deserved to party it up on his birthday. He'd become a man that Gage was proud of, one that their father would've been proud of too.

Shaking off his melancholy thoughts, he joined in the coarse banter as the balls were racked and the tournament got started. He tried to focus on the game but his mind, and his gaze, kept wandering back to the bar and the fetching woman behind it.

Her curves were generous in all the right places and she wasn't shy about showing them off. Dressed in a thin top that clung to fantastic tits and a pair of tight jeans that drew his gaze to a butt that begged to be spanked, she was definitely sexy.

"Wipe your chin, big brother, you're starting to drool."

Gage pulled his gaze away from the lady and shrugged. "I'm just enjoying the scenery. No big deal."

Garret flashed him a knowing smirk. "If by enjoying the scenery you mean eyeing her like a hungry man eyes a prime rib dinner, you're right. That's what you're doing."

Gage ignored him and watched their opponent sink another shot on the pool table. It shouldn't bother him that he couldn't keep his eyes off the sassy bartender, but it did.

There'd been a time when he wouldn't even consider walking away from a woman like that. A time when he'd only been interested in casual relationships and good times. But things had changed.

He'd shifted career tracks, with an eye towards settling down, and bought a fantastic old house in need of some tender loving care. Now he just needed a good woman who shared his vision of the future to round out the picture. Not a night of bedroom acrobatics with some good time girl he met in a bar.

The only problem with that theory was the nice girls he'd been dating for the past six months were a bit boring.

"Gage!" Garret shouted at him from across the table. "It's your turn, man. I set it up for you. All you have to do now is clear the table."

He fixed his eyes on the pool table, actually seeing it this time. There were three balls left, all lined up perfectly. Six ball in the corner pocket, bring it back for the four ball in the side, and then on to the eight in the corner. Easy.

He bent over the table and lined up his shot. The guys around him jeered at him, trying to throw him off.

Pulling back his hand, he let it go, effortlessly sending the six to the corner. Straightening up, he glanced over his shoulder and saw the woman herself watching him.

Had she been checking out his ass?

He could see an embarrassed flush bloom in her cheeks from where he was. But that didn't stop a naughty smile from spreading across her luscious lips as she wiggled her fingers at him.

He shook his head and fought back a grin. He tried to concentrate on the game as he walked around the table, but it was tough. Bending forward, he lined up the cue carefully before smoothly taking the shot. And watched as the four ball sailed into the cushion, not even coming close to the pocket.

The boys hooted at him, jeering at him for missing such an easy shot. How the hell did he miss that?

He glanced at the bar again. Easily. He'd been distracted by the image of those full red lips wrapped around his dick.

With a shake of his head, he chuckled. Was it truly that surprising she distracted him? After all, he'd always had a soft spot for bad girls...or a hard-on. Depending on how you looked at it.

He picked up his beer bottle and drained the last bit before moving towards the bar. What the hell? What could a little flirting hurt?

Ɏ Ɏ Ɏ Ɏ

Sable walked up and down the length of the bar. She stopped to chat here and there as she made sure everyone's drinks were full and no one was left waiting for service. Miranda had gone home, leaving the pub in her hands for the night. But before she'd left, Miranda had extracted a promise to get together that weekend for a much-needed bonding session.

Unable to keep her gaze away from the pool tables for very long, Sable looked over and got an eyeful of faded denim, tight across firm buttocks. The sexy bad ass, the one they called Gage, bent over to make another shot, and she couldn't peel her eyes away from the sight of his awesome butt. Until he straightened up, glanced over his shoulder, and caught her staring.

Infusing her smile with sassiness, she gave him a small wave and went back to work.

It was a real chore for her to concentrate when all she wanted to do was watch him move around the table. His movements were slow and deliberate, yet they had an inherent sensuality to them. A sensuality her photographer's eye told her would come through on film.

The way he held the pool cue and smoothly stroked it through his fingers to make the balls go wherever he wanted. Her belly tightened at the thought of his hands stroking her that same way, and she let out a sigh of longing.

Someone put money in the jukebox, and she sang along with ZZ Top as she strolled down the bar, picking up empties and pouring replacements. She was listening to Bruce, one of the regulars, tell a joke when she felt her skin tighten and her nipples harden.

With a quick glance to the left, she saw Gage leaning against the bar, watching her.

Deep breaths, she told herself. Bruce finished his joke, and she laughed along with him even though she hadn't heard a word he'd said.

She picked up the empty glass from in front of him and sauntered towards Gage, her eyes glued to his the whole time.

"Hi there."

The bonfire in her belly spread lower and she felt her body soften, moisten. Struggling to ignore the inner heat, she tried to treat him like any other customer.

Any other customer who just happened to make her nipples stand at attention with just a look.

"Another beer?"

"Sure." He handed her a bill and took the proffered bottle.

Like the self-conscious adolescent of her past, she struggled for something to say. It was more than his good looks that got to her; she dealt with good-looking men every day. It was *him*. The vibe of tightly leashed power that radiated off him called to something primal inside her.

She couldn't decide whether to run away from him as fast as she could, or strip off her clothes and howl, "Take me!" at the top of her lungs.

What the hell? She'd never run from a challenge in her life. She wasn't going to start now.

"How's the pool tournament going?"

"Not so good for me," he chuckled.

"Why do I find that hard to believe?"

"I don't know. Why do you?" A twinkle gleamed in his dark eyes.

"Something tells me you're good at whatever you do. When you want to be, anyway." She leaned her elbows on the bar, showing off her cleavage. "Maybe you just need the right incentive to have a better game."

"Could be." The corners of his lips twitched. "What do you suppose that would be?"

"Umm, I'm not sure." She was drowning in those potent eyes of his and her mind had all but shut down. "Motivation is an individual thing."

"Well, when you think of something that might motivate me, let me know." He rapped his knuckles on the bar, gave her a crooked smile, and walked away.

Oh boy!

She let her head drop to the bar and sucked air deep into her lungs.

Maybe she'd bitten off more than she could chew. Her heart pounded, and her skin itched in a way that could only be scratched by a man's touch. A touch that she hadn't felt in a long time.

"Maybe it's time to do something about that," she muttered to herself as she wiped down the bar.

With another glance at where Gage now stood surrounded by rowdy men at the pool tables, Sable made a decision. She knew she would never take off while Miranda needed her to keep the pub going, so she was going to be stuck in this city for a while. She'd need something to take the edge of her never-ending restlessness. A hot affair with a sexy hunk like him just might do the trick.

"Sable! I need some drinks down here." Katie's voice broke into her lust-filled thoughts.

"Sorry, Katie. Got a bit distracted there."

"Don't blame you." She glanced over her shoulder at the room full of men. "I'm having a hard time not slipping into fantasyland myself. Or...am I already in fantasyland with all these good-looking men?"

Sable laughed and began to fill Katie's order. "There does seem to be an unusual amount of hot guys in here tonight, doesn't there? Find any one in particular that gets your juices flowing?"

"The blonde at table five. My God, he has gorgeous eyes! Every time he looks at me, my mind goes blank." She laughed at herself and gave Sable an embarrassed smile. "I had to go back and ask what it was he'd ordered because I was five steps from the table when I realized I couldn't remember."

Sable knew the feeling. Looking into Gage's eyes had made her own mind go blank and left her feeling as young and tongue-tied as Katie. Something she had no intention of letting happen again. She prided herself on her ability to be able to talk to anyone.

That was one of the reasons she loved bartending so much. It took all kinds to make the world go around, and almost every kind walked into a bar at one point or another. Most people hated working night shifts, but not Sable. A whole different world existed when the sun went down, a sub-culture she felt at home in.

She reached into the cooler and pulled out another frosted mug. She filled it with draft and placed in front of Jim, another regular, before he had a chance to ask.

"Thanks, sweetheart," he said absentmindedly as he listened intently to one of Bruce's fishing tales.

She smiled and started to fill the dishwasher with dirty glasses. It hadn't taken long for her to outgrow the sleep all day, party all night lifestyle. Fun as it was when she was younger, nowadays it wasn't safe, or smart, to live like that. Plus, she'd found other ways to feed her seeker's soul.

She'd traveled the world, had a black belt in karate, could drive anything with two or more wheels and prepare a gourmet meal for six with only two hours notice. But her real passion was photography.

The ability to combine her wanderlust with her devotion to picture-taking kept her from feeling lost. She loved to travel all over and take pictures of the people she met, the places she saw. She knew it was a bit bohemian, but she wasn't close to her family, had no steady man in her life, and no real reason to stay in any one place for any longer than she desired. So she took advantage of being able to live the gypsy-style life and went wherever her heart led her.

Sometimes she dreamed about having her own photography show. She'd even had some commercial success with travel magazines and agencies that liked her particular style of work. She had been in South Africa, working on an idea for a theme show, when she'd received Miranda's cry for help. Without hesitation, she'd stuck her camera back into her backpack and headed home to help her only true friend out.

The afternoon heat had dissipated into a warm summer evening and not only had the regulars come in, but a lot of street traffic as well. Some people came in to enjoy the air conditioning, but others preferred to sit on the patio and have a few drinks as the temperatures dropped. The small pub wasn't at its full capacity of two hundred people, but they were busy enough that Sable was kept running with filling orders for Katie and entertaining the regulars who occupied the bar stools.

The jukebox spit out classic rock that could just be heard over the din of conversation and laughter, and the air crackled with the energy of the eclectic crowd. Sable stopped for a second just to soak it all up.

"Finally have a minute to breathe, huh?"

Jake, the cook, climbed onto a barstool in front of Sable and she glanced at the clock. One a.m. already. The night had flown by. The kitchen was now closed, and Jake was ready for his nightly beer.

Together they looked over the crowd before Sable turned her attention to him. With dark blonde hair cut close to his skull, dressed in cargo pants and a black T-shirt, Jake didn't look like a typical cook. Instead, he looked like he should be running around in fatigues, toting a sniper rifle.

His loose nondescript clothes did nothing to hide his firm biceps or lean, fit body. *Funny how the sight of Jake's muscles never made my knees go weak. Not like Gage's could.*

Sable laughed at herself. Women hit on Jake regularly, and she'd watched him turn them all down as gently as he could. Absurdly good-looking though he was, he didn't spark even a flicker of heat in her belly. Something about him made her very aware of her femininity, and at the same time, warned her off.

Since the first night they'd worked together, a sort of unspoken alliance had been made. Each of them recognized the kindred soul of another loner, someone who kept their own thoughts and feelings to themselves. While they were friendly, neither reached out to the other in an effort to deepen their association.

"Yeah, it's a rush when a group comes in, especially one that's all men with an excuse to party," she said with a grin. "They've been here all night but they seem like a good bunch, so there shouldn't be any problems."

Without asking what he wanted, Sable reached into a cooler, pulled out a bottle, and placed it in front of him.

"Nah. The one with the funny hat on is Garret Dougherty. Him and his buddies go to the university during the winter and work with forest fire crews in the summer. Whenever they've got time off, they come back into town to let loose. You'll never have a hard time with them and you'll get to know them pretty well if you stick around. They're good guys. But him." Jake nodded toward where a head full of unruly dark hair was bent over the pool table, lining up a shot. "He's an unknown."

"His name's Gage." Sable watched as with a quick flick of his wrist Gage shot the cue ball across the table, knocking a striped ball into the corner pocket.

She saw Jake eyeing her shrewdly. "What? I overheard them when he came in."

When he didn't comment further, she felt her cheeks heat up and hoped they weren't turning pink. "He's nothing I can't handle, I'm sure," she said with confidence.

"Uh-huh." Jake looked at her a moment longer before taking a long drink from his beer. Just how much could he see from the kitchen?

It was time to turn the tables on him.

"What about you? No hot date after work tonight?" she teased. She knew he would sit at the bar until the pub was empty. No matter how many how times she'd told him she could handle any problems that cropped up, he still stuck around until the last straggler left. He was protective that way, and strangely, it didn't annoy her.

"Actually, I have a hot date with Michelle Pfeiffer and a bowl of popcorn. But she'll wait for me," he said arrogantly.

"But will she be alone while she waits for you? Who's she with tonight? Robert Redford? Sean Penn?"

"Don't forget Jack!" Jim weighed in from the stool next to Jake. "You can't forget Jack Nicholson. He had her and Cher going at the same time. Susan Sarandon, too!"

"It's Harrison Ford tonight."

"Stiff competition, Jake." Sable laughed as she emptied the glass washer. "Indiana Jones captured my heart years ago."

"I'm not interested in her heart." Jake flashed a wicked grin and laughed.

"But when you catch their heart...you get the best of them. Or so I'm told."

They turned in silence to the newcomer and Sable's heart thumped against her rib cage. Suddenly aware of Bryan Adams in the background asking if you've ever really loved a woman, Sable found herself wanting to know if this man ever had.

"Do you believe everything you're told?" Jake broke the silence.

"Only when I'm offered up proof as well," replied the man who had been wreaking havoc with her hormones all night. He looked at Sable. "Think of anything that might motivate me yet?"

"Huh? Oh!" Give your head a shake, girl!

Pulling herself together, she gave him her naughtiest smile. "I've got a few ideas."

"Care to share them with me?"

"Not quite yet," she teased. "Maybe if you're still around when I'm done closing up..."

Jake's eyebrows shot up, and she knew her words had shocked him. They had worked together six nights a week since she'd started there a few months ago, and he'd seen her flirt with everything in pants. But he also knew she always went home alone.

She started to empty the dishwasher and put the clean glasses away, not looking at Jake or Gage. She knew Jake had noticed her special interest in this guy earlier; now she'd just confirmed it. This guy was different.

Special.

ΥΥΥΥ

Gage watched the playful bartender as she worked and thought about her invitation. It was subtle, but he knew a come-on when he heard one.

He was surprised to find himself tempted by it. That was wrong—the invitation didn't tempt him. She did. He felt the heat of a steady gaze on him and glanced sideways to lock eyes with the man who had been talking when he stepped up to the bar.

"You with Garret and his group?" he asked.

"He's my little brother. The name's Gage." He held out his hand to the stranger.

"Jake." The men measured each other as they shook hands. "I haven't played pool in a while. How about you and me go have a game?"

"Sure. Go on up there. I'll just grab another drink." Gage reached into his pocket for money to pay for the beer already being pulled from the cooler. The sexy lady set the bottle on the bar and reached for the money. When she tried to lift the cash off the bar, he pinned it there with a firm finger.

She lifted her eyes questioningly to his and waited.

"And you are?" he asked.

"Sable," she answered, a smile spreading across her juicy red lips and lighting up her baby blue eyes. "And I'll be here when you're done with your game."

ΥΥΥΥ

Sable pushed open the door to her tiny apartment and dragged herself inside. God, what a night!

Jake and Gage had played pool until the bar was cleaned up and everyone else had gone home, including Katie. They were still playing when Sable had gone into the back office to lock up the money and shut down the computers.

She'd taken a few minutes to fluff her hair and check her make-up before going back out to join them, only to find Gage gone and Jake alone.

She knew he could see her disappointment but he didn't say anything, and she refused to ask. They were silent while she locked the doors. With a final goodnight, she'd climbed on her mountain bike and used the ten-block ride home to burn off her excess energy.

Dropping her satchel in the entryway, she went straight to the bathroom and pushed aside the shower curtain. With a quick twist on each handle, the water pummeled the empty tub. Steam filled the small room while she shed her work clothes, stepped under the spray, and let out a low moan of satisfaction as the hot water hit her between the shoulder blades.

Eyes closed, she tilted her head back and let the water flatten her curls to her head before streaming down her body. The shower filled with the smell of the stale smoke releasing from her hair. Without opening her eyes, she reached for the shampoo and lathered up. Soon the air was fresh and fruity and she let her mind wander as she went about her routine.

Gage consumed her thoughts and tendrils of anger heated her blood. She shouldn't care that some sexy stranger didn't have the decency to say goodnight. Shoving her head under the spray, she rinsed away the shampoo before filling her palms with conditioner and covering her hair in the creamy lotion. She left it in to soak and ran a sudsy sponge over her body.

Languorous pleasure edged past the anger and her nipples hardened. The same way they had when Gage had walked into the pub. Her body seemed to wake up around him, as if it recognized him. Never before had a man affected her so strongly, so immediately.

Never before had a man walked away from her after she'd offered up an invitation, no matter how subtle.

She turned in the shower so the brusque jets of water landed directly on her chest. She ran her hands over her breasts and groaned at the feelings quickening her pulse. While she didn't believe in casual sex, she did believe in casual relationships based on sex. And it had been far too long since she'd enjoyed one.

The arousal flowing through her at the thought of getting naked with Gage made her wonder how his hands would feel skimming over her skin. Would he be rough? Or gentle? Would he be firm and passionate, or slow and sensuous?

Imagining it was his hands cupping her breasts, she tweaked her nipples and let her eyes slide closed. She leaned against the tile wall and slipped her other hand between her thighs. Teasing herself, she slid a finger over lips plump with arousal and felt the thick wetness there.

Her fingertip brushed against her hard button and her breath caught.

Knees weakening, she focused on that sensitive nub of flesh. Flicking her finger back and forth, she forgot about the way the night had ended and concentrated on the pleasure gathering low in her belly.

The image of him bent over the pool table flashed through her mind, morphing into one of him bent over her, splayed out on the pool table. His dark eyes gleaming with wicked delight as he watched her please herself. The thought of doing it for him, of him watching her, pushed her over the edge. She pressed the palm of her hand against her core and rocked her body until her orgasm faded.

Hands hanging limply by her sides, she remembered her subtlety earlier that night and made a promise it wouldn't happen again. She was twenty-nine year old woman who went after what she wanted in life. And she wanted Gage.

Chapter Three

"I don't get it."

"Get what?" Sable asked from her spot on the floor.

"The whole 'want to be bad' thing. What do you mean bad? And why him?" Miranda shifted her position on the overstuffed couch, concern stamped clearly on her delicate features.

They were lounging around Miranda's apartment sharing a lazy Sunday afternoon and a bottle of wine, when the conversation inevitably turned to men. Gage, in particular.

"Why him? Why not him?" Sable held up empty hands. "I'm twenty-nine years old, and I've never even been on a 'real' date, Mandy. Men don't want to date me, they like the way I look, and they want to fuck me. It's about time I turn it around and chase a man I want."

"Sable!" Miranda's voice rang with disapproval.

"What?" She sighed. "You know what I'm saying is true. How many times have you seen a man ask me out to dinner, or a movie? Never. Well, okay, there was Tom, but he was married so we both know dinner wasn't what he was really after. No matter what I do, men look at me and see someone they want to have a good time with, not someone they want to take home to meet Mom. And now I've found a guy I want to wrestle around between the sheets with, so why shouldn't I go for it?"

"How do you know you won't get hurt?"

"I don't need to worry about that. I'll never let him get that close."

"How do you know that?" Miranda asked. "You can't predict what happens when emotions get involved, Sable."

Sable looked at her best friend in exasperation. "Who said emotions will get involved? You're the one who's always telling me how thick my walls are, how I never let anyone get to know the real me."

"Not the real you, the *whole* you. You're too honest to not let people know the real you. You just never let them see the whole picture. You only let them see what you think they want to see and keep the rest hidden. It's almost as if you think they won't like you if you let them discover too much."

"That's not true!" She gave her friend a cocky grin. "How could anyone not like me?"

She dodged the pillow Miranda snatched off the couch and threw at her. "Seriously though. I want him, Mandy . . .there's no denying it. He's the first man in a long time to get my juices going with just a look. *And* I'm more than ready for a fling with a tall, dark, and sexy stranger."

Sable got off the floor and flopped onto the sofa before reaching for her glass of wine. They were trying an Australian Chardonnay and it wasn't half-bad.

"Sable!" Miranda frowned at her and then dissolved into giggles. "You are so bad."

"That's what I'm saying! He makes me want to be bad. So bad that I sort of invited him to go home with me after work last night." She cringed, knowing her friend wouldn't understand her behavior.

"You asked him to go home with you?" Miranda squeaked, her eyebrows now hidden under her bangs.

"Not straight out like that. I was subtle; too subtle obviously since he was gone when I came out of the back office. He didn't even say good night."

"Maybe it wasn't that you were too subtle, Sable, maybe he just wasn't interested." Mandy said it so gently Sable knew her friend was trying not to hurt her feelings.

"Oh, he was interested. I have no doubt about that." And she didn't. There was no way she'd misread the heat that made the air vibrate between them.

"What?" She asked, noticing a weird look flicker across Miranda's face.

"Nothing." She sighed. "Sometimes I just wish I had your confidence."

Sable laughed derisively. "If there's one thing I'm confident about in this world, it's that all men are interested in is sex and sports."

"With an attitude like that I don't get why you're even considering this. Don't you want more from a man than sex? You don't know anything about this guy, except that he looks good in his Levi's."

"Just because you're waiting for love doesn't mean I have to." Sable shrugged her shoulders nonchalantly. "Some people are meant to be loved and live happily ever after. Some aren't." She raised her head and pointed her chin at Miranda. "You'll find love and live happily ever after, Mandy. You deserve to have everything you want out of life."

A flash of sadness welled in Sable's chest but she tamped it down and smiled confidently. But her friend knew her too well to be fooled.

Miranda reached for her hand, where it lay across the back of the couch. "So do you. I don't know why you won't believe that."

They looked at each other for a moment before Sable let out a belch that spoiled the moment. Their giggles ended the heartfelt portion of the night, and conversation restarted. Jumping from fashion to movies, they avoided anything serious and finished off the bottle of wine.

"What do you want for dinner?" Miranda called out from the kitchen where she retrieved their second bottle from the fridge. "Chinese or pizza?"

"Pizza! I haven't had a decent pizza in months." Her mouth watered at the thought of a cheesy pepperoni and mushroom pizza.

"Pizza's ordered." Miranda returned to the room carrying plates, napkins, and cutlery as well as the wine. "What was your favorite dish while you were in South Africa?"

"Salad."

"Salad?"

"Yup. I ate salad almost every day."

"You? Queen of the carbohydrate cravings?"

Sable laughed. "Yeah, I know! But the family I was staying with made this incredible salad with sprouts and avocados with only vinegar for dressing. It was weird . . . but that's what I craved when I was there. I figured it had something to do with the heat there. The temperatures were pretty hot for a Canadian girl and cooking was not my favorite thing to do."

It was so nice to just sit and relax with Miranda. They hadn't really had a chance for girl talk since Sable had returned to Edmonton almost a month and a half ago. All of their conversations had been about the pub and getting Miranda up to speed on how things were done in the industry.

Miranda's job as a legal secretary hadn't prepared her for running a pub. Sable got the impression that Jake had been a big help too. He'd taken over the food orders and anything else to do with the kitchen before Sable'd even arrived back in the city.

"Tell me about Jake." Sable commanded.

"What's to tell? He came with the pub."

"What do you mean?"

"Uncle Tom's will had a provision in it for Jake. Nothing much, just that he be allowed to live above the pub and work there for as long as he wanted. Now, forget about the pub," she instructed. "Tell me about South Africa."

Sable closed her eyes and let her mind flow back six weeks in time. She described the beaches and markets, talked about the people she met in the hostels while she bummed around before stopping at The Backpacker's Hideaway.

"I only planned to stay there for two nights and ended up staying for five. When I was checking out on the fifth day, I had the urge to ask if they needed any help. They told me about the lack of teachers at the township school and offered me free room and board if I volunteered to teach there. So I stayed."

She knew from the way her friend watched her that Miranda was envious of her adventures. But what Miranda didn't know was that she was envious of Miranda's stable life and the knowledge that she had somewhere she belonged. People always wanted what they didn't have. It was human nature.

The pizza arrived and the two women ate—Sable digging in with gusto while Miranda daintily used her silverware to cut her pizza and eat small pieces instead of big bites. They giggled like teenagers, discussed celebrity gossip, and finished off the second bottle of wine.

When both were lying contentedly on the floor Sable glanced at the clock. Seven o'clock.

"Time for me to head home. I hear a big load of laundry calling my name." She climbed to her feet and pulled Miranda up next to her. "C'mon Mandy, you need to work some of this off too, so you can walk me half-way home."

They headed out of the little house and started down the street. It was a quiet Sunday evening. The sun was still out, but the evening air had turned humid in the heat. An old man sat on the front porch of one house, smoking his pipe and watching the passers-by. At another, a middle-aged woman weeded her flower garden while her husband mowed the lawn, sweat dripping down his face. He looked like he was going to keel over any minute. Sable and Miranda were quiet, each with their own thoughts as they walked.

A few blocks from Miranda's house, they approached a community park. Sable noticed the kids that had been playing on the swings earlier were gone and the small grassy area now held a small group of men playing football. Some were shirtless, showing off plenty of muscles.

She nudged Miranda in the ribs and nodded at the fit male bodies running around. When they got closer, Sable noticed a particular hard body topped with a dark head of hair, and her heart thumped in recognition.

"It's Gage," she said.

"And Jake," added Miranda.

They shared an eloquent look before heading over to the group of sweaty men. Football was the game that had brought the women together as kids.

The play stopped when Gage tackled Garret and both of them went down in a tangle of arms and legs. The men's yelling and laugher made the women smile as they stopped close to them.

Unable to resist, she called out to them. "Can anybody join in?"

Ƴ Ƴ Ƴ Ƴ

Disentangling himself from his little brother, Gage stood up. And saw Jake standing with a couple of women.

One very sexy one that he thought he wouldn't ever see again.

His eyes roamed over Sable's bare legs and visions of them wrapped around his waist filled his head.

Down, boy.

While his mind knew he was looking for more than a sexual relationship, his body obviously hadn't gotten the message yet. He closed his eyes briefly and tried to keep his cock from standing at attention.

"Fancy seeing you all here," Sable said.

Gage saw her shoot Jake an accusing look, which he answered with a smile. Was there something going on between them?

The group of six men took advantage of the ladies' interruption to retrieve their drinks and gulp gratefully from various plastic bottles. Gage picked his up from next to his gym bag and twisted off the cap. After taking a drink of water, he tipped the bottle over his head and felt the cool wetness seep into his hair, dripping down his face and neck. Not quite a cold shower, but it would have to do.

Shaking the water from his hair and eyes, he looked over at Sable and felt a punch of raw lust hit him in the gut at the hungry look in her eyes. His heartbeat sped up and he fought to keep his dick from swelling to embarrassing proportions. There was no way he would cool down if she kept looking at him like that!

She pulled her gaze from his and turned to Garret. "Seems like your party has trimmed by a few members since last night. Miranda and I would love to join this one." Miranda nodded in agreement, and Gage watched his brother stick his foot in his mouth.

"But girls don't play football."

"Some girls do." Sable's eyes narrowed and she planted her hands on those rounded hips of hers.

"Of course, you're welcome to join us. The more the merrier." Gage spoke up before his brother could insult the women any further. "It's only a touch game, so no one will get hurt." He cast a menacing look at the others, making them aware they better treat the women with care.

The cold water over his head had done nothing to dispel the images flashing through his mind of just how he would prefer to work up a sweat with Sable. Thinking it best to keep his distance, he sent her to join Jake and Garret's team and invited Miranda to join his own.

Sable looked disappointed, but Gage figured it was for the best. He didn't realize that being on the opposing team had its own pitfalls.

His team had possession of the ball, and after a brief huddle, they lined up. The plan was to use the men to guard Miranda while she ran for the touchdown. He hoped she could catch the ball.

Gage caught the snap, and the action was on. While Sable, Tim, and Jake tried to get past the defense and intercept the ball, Garret covered Miranda as she ran up the field for the pass. Gage let the ball fly at the same time Sable broke through the defense and jumped on him. They went down hard, with her landing on top to a loud "Oomph!" as the air whooshed from his lungs.

Gage opened his eyes and laughed. So much for keeping her at a safe distance.

She braced her hands on the grass next to his shoulders and levered herself into position, straddling his hips. She looked down at him with a wide grin and a gleam in her eyes.

"This is *touch* football, Sable, not tackle." He tried to sound put out.

"I am touching you." Sable wiggled her hips over his groin and looked at him in mock innocence.

His large hands rested on her thighs, and he groaned softly. "You're incorrigible, aren't you?"

Sitting up, he gripped her hips and lifted her off of him before she noticed that he'd finally lost the battle with his dick.

She rose gracefully to her feet and smiled down at him. "And you love it, don't you?"

God help him, he did.

"You are fast!" Jay's excited voice pulled Gage back to the game at hand.

Tearing his gaze from Sable's delicious ass, he watched his teammates jog up to him—Ron on one side of Miranda and Jay on the other. Both were laughing and slapping her on the back.

"That was beautiful! Did you see the look on Garret's face? He looked like he just ran against Ben Johnson!"

Gage realized Miranda had scored a touchdown while he had been distracted with a lap full of soft curves.

Excellent. It would do his little brother some good to get shown up by a woman. The boy was getting far too arrogant.

The game continued as daylight started to dim. The women fast became as sweaty and disheveled as the men, but never complained. Laughter and veiled schoolyard insults peppered the air as the teams battled for supremacy in a close race.

Sable didn't tackle him again, but she did take the opportunity to slap him on the butt in congratulations when he threw another touchdown pass. She laughed when Jake yelled at her for consorting with the enemy, then ran a pattern that shook off everyone to score the tying goal for her own team.

She'd been tenacious when she went after that touchdown, and Gage wondered if she was that way with everything she went after. She would probably be an animal in bed. A sleek, sexy, wild animal that would wring him dry.

God, he was a masochist for even considering it. But he couldn't erase the images from his brain.

In the final play, Jake threw the ball to Garret, who caught it in a beautiful mid-air stretch that came down on the other side of the makeshift goal posts, winning the game for their team. The cheers were raucous amid the backslapping and high fives while they rubbed it in to the others.

"And you said girls can't play football!" Sable punched Garret in the shoulder.

"I didn't say can't, I said don't," he admitted sheepishly. "I may be young, but I know better than to try and tell a woman she can't do something."

"Only because you know Mom would never let you get away with it." Gage chimed in.

"Damn right. I'm not stupid!"

The group laughed at that and started to gather their things.

"Got any plans for the rest of the night?"

He looked up to see that Sable had made her way through the group and now stood next to him. She'd asked him quietly while the others continued chatting about the game.

"Just a good meal and a hot shower." He shoved his arms and head through the holes of a clean T-shirt and yanked it over his chest. He couldn't stop a grin from forming when she sighed at the sight of his disappearing abs.

The she raised her gaze back to his and smiled mischievously. "Really? That's exactly what I had in mind too. Want some company?"

He laughed softly. She was something else. How was he supposed to resist her? She was beautiful, confident, sexy, and obviously horny. Everything he had always asked for in a woman.

Only now he wanted more. Now he wanted a woman who was ready to settle down. Someone he could raise a family with, not just someone to have a good time with.

He studied her smiling face and gave in. "How about I give you a ride home, and we leave the rest for another time?"

"It's a start."

Ƭ Ƭ Ƭ Ƭ

They said their good-byes to everyone, and Gage steered her toward the vehicles parked nearby. When he stopped next to a yellow Dodge Dakota, Sable laughed out loud.

"What?"

"You just happen to have the truck of my dreams." She threw a wink at him. "Think it means anything?"

He opened the door for her and waited while she climbed in, his lips tilted in a small smile, but not saying a word. While he walked around to his side, she saw Miranda climb into Jake's Jeep and felt relieved her friend didn't have to walk home alone in the deepening twilight.

Gage opened the driver's door, tossed his bag behind the seat, and climbed in. She breathed deeply as his scent filled the small confines of the truck cab, and lust unfurled in her belly.

An image of him standing naked, still dripping from a shower, burst into her mind. She licked her lips and pressed her thighs together at the thought of licking those water droplets off him.

The truck engine turned over, and with a start Sable realized Gage was looking at her expectantly.

"Hi," she said.

"Hi there," he responded after a moment of silence. "I need your address."

Ugh! Feeling like an idiot, she gave him directions to her apartment. Before she could get too distracted by the sight of his bare, muscular thighs so close to her own, she asked the question foremost in her mind.

"So, where did you disappear to last night?"

"It was late when Jake and I finished our game, so I thought it best just to go home."

"And you invited him to play ball with you guys tonight?" *He'd made plans with Jake instead of her?*

His hands fidgeted on the steering wheel, the muscles in his forearms jumped, and so did her pulse rate. She'd never found a man's forearms sexy before.

"Yeah. Our talk turned to ball, and he mentioned he used to play so I invited him along. Are you and he very close?"

"Me and Jake?" she squawked.

Gage laughed at her surprise. "Yes, you and Jake."

"Not really, no. I mean we work together almost every night, and we get along good. But we've never really talked. We've never had the need to."

"What do you mean 'the need to'?"

"Well, he runs the kitchen, and I handle the bar. We each do our thing, and everything goes smoothly. Why?" Was he jealous? Did he really think she would hit on him if she had something going with Jake?

"No reason, really." He shrugged. "He just seemed pretty protective of you last night, so I wondered. Here we are." He slowed the truck to a stop and put the parking brake on.

Sable's brain was still stuck on needs. All the naughty needs that had started to build inside her the moment he'd stepped into the pub. The need to taste him, to feel him. To have his hands cup her breasts, his fingers pinch her nipples, his tongue in her mouth, his cock buried deep inside her.

"Would you like to come in?" she asked, her voice husky.

He grimaced, as if in pain, when he answered her. "I better not."

"I'll feed you." When she saw him hesitate, she continued to tempt him. "I make a mean chicken stir fry. As long as you like it hot and spicy."

Heat flashed in his eyes at that, and Sable felt a shiver run down her spine.

"Hot is definitely a favorite of mine, but I have to say no thanks." He studied her intently for a beat and then continued. "Look, Sable, you're a beautiful and intriguing woman, but I'm at a place in my life right now where I want more than a casual relationship. And I get the feeling that's all you're looking for. So . . . I think it's best if we just leave things the way they are."

Just her luck. She finally decided she wanted to have hot fling, and the guy she wanted to do it with is looking for a relationship.

She'd consider a relationship, if she didn't suck at them. But she could barely handle a relationship with her family and they *had* to love her.

She looked into the depths of his eyes. His desire was clear. His words might have told her he didn't want her, but his eyes told her he was lying, and she felt the rightness of *them* in her gut.

Determined not to let him go without something to think about, she reached a hand up to cup his cheek and softly pressed her lips against his.

She'd meant it to be a quick kiss, a tease, but the instant their lips touched, hunger swamped her. She ran her tongue across his full bottom lip, seeking entrance. His lips parted and his tongue darted out to duel with hers. Sliding her fingers into his hair, she pulled him closer and deepened the kiss. Her heart thumped against her chest, her breathing became ragged and all thoughts fled as they tasted each other for the first time.

Needing air, she pulled back a bit, nibbled at his lips, and kissed the corner of his mouth before sealing her lips over his fully once more. When his hand cupped the back of her head, she tightened her grip on his hair and pulled her mouth away. My God, she was practically on top of him!

She rested her forehead against his as their panting breaths mingled in the small space between them. She looked into his eyes and felt her chest tighten with a foreign emotion.

"If you change your mind, you know where to find me." Not bothering to keep her disappointment from showing, she pulled away completely and exited the truck before she said something she'd really regret.

Something like "Take a chance on me."

Chapter Four

Gage watched her hips sway as she walked up the path and bit down on a groan of frustration at her saucy wave goodbye. Shifting in his seat, he adjusted himself inside his shorts and stared out the window at nothing.

Not long ago, he would've followed her inside for dinner, a hot shower, and anything else she offered. But all that had changed. He couldn't let himself get distracted by a woman that made his cock hard with just a kiss when what he really wanted was a woman who could be his best friend, share his dreams, and raise his kids with love and security.

He'd always avoided women looking for commitment, and now that he wanted one, he couldn't find one. Or he could find one, but not one he *wanted*. He wanted Sable. Being near her made him feel... something, when he hadn't felt anything towards a woman in a long time.

But she didn't want anything more than sex.

Putting the truck in gear, he headed home, consumed with thoughts of her. Their role reversal was a bit unsettling. He'd turned down women before and never thought twice about it. He hoped he didn't regret it this time.

And why wasn't she interested in more? In the bar, he'd thought she was just a party girl. But now, he got the impression there was more to her than met the eye. He had no concrete reason to think that was true. Hell, maybe it was just his subconscious trying to find a way to see her again. He'd truly enjoyed having her, and Miranda, join their football game. Sable's sass and attitude appealed to him immensely. *But could there be more to her that?*

He knew his looks appealed to women; he'd never had any trouble getting laid, or getting dates. Women, by and large, found forestry men sexy. Especially the ones who worked the fire brigade. But he didn't do that anymore, either. He'd started work as a Forest-Fire Fighter because it was the best paying job he could get when he was eighteen and fresh from high school. He'd wanted to help his mom out with the bills, and he'd been able to that.

Then the job grew into a career. He'd become addicted to the adrenaline rush of fighting forest fires, but after thirteen years, the excitement had begun to wane. He'd shifted his interest to other aspects of forestry and jumped at the chance to be an Environmental Investigator.

His plan to settle down was falling right into place. Going after people who abused the land and its resources was a stimulating new line of work—a job that utilized his brain, his instincts, and his love for the land. Plus, he now lived in the city, in his own house. Which put him closer to his family, but not too close. The only part of the plan that wasn't falling into place was the nice girl to take home to Mom.

ϓ ϓ ϓ ϓ

Early Monday afternoon Gage strolled into the University of Alberta science lab and set the case of water samples on the counter top. The blonde in the lab coat behind the counter turned at the sound and frowned at him.

"These are the samples your department requested from Alberta Environment," he explained.

"Oh!" She pulled her hands out of her pockets and reached for the box with a light chuckle. "Thank you. I've been expecting these, although you don't look like the interns they usually use as delivery boys."

He looked down at his pressed khakis, button-down dress shirt, and tie and agreed with her. "I'm Gage Dougherty." He held out a hand to her and explained that he was a new investigator with the regional office, and since he was near the University anyway, he'd offered to drop them off.

"Dr. Jane Smith," she replied as she held onto his hand for a second longer than necessary.

He got the distinct impression she was interested in him, but she wouldn't meet his gaze for more than a second or two. Unlike Sable, who tempted him with a wicked sparkle in her baby blues.

Maybe that was a good thing.

He chatted with her for a bit, making small talk and debating if he should ask her out or not. She seemed like a very nice, smart woman. The kind that would be interested in a real relationship. She gave every indication that she would say yes, but the invitation never left his mouth. Instead, as soon as he had directions to the new photography exhibit, he left the room with a casual smile and a wave.

His friend Darren had entered a few pictures from some of the fires he'd worked earlier that summer in the university's contest, and Gage had told him he would drop by and check them out. Vote on them if he could, since the contest was supposed to be a viewer's choice.

As he strode across the campus, he kicked himself in the ass for not asking Jane for her number. She seemed like a nice girl. Just what he wanted. He'd go back after checking out Darren's pictures. Maybe she'd be free to go for coffee.

Spotting the correct entrance, he pulled open the glass doors and headed for the photography department. He slowed his pace as he entered the exhibit room and checked out the pictures.

Close-ups of flowers, your standard waterfall, a skyline. Pretty boring stuff. Finally he saw a small area with Darren's name posted above it. Then he saw who was looking at them and his pulse jumped.

Swaying back and forth on her feet was the one woman he was trying not to run into. Shiny curls tumbled down her back making his fingers itch with the need to tangle his hands in them, and tight black dress pants cupped the butt that had been in his dreams the night before. He watched as she shifted her bag on her shoulder, cocking her head first to one side then the other.

He should turn around and return another time. He should go back to the science building and ask Jane out for a coffee. Instead, he let his feet lead him inexorably closer to her.

"Beautiful, isn't it?"

Clutching her chest as if to hold her pounding heart in, Sable turned and looked at him in surprise. Standing next to her, he picked up on a subtle scent, one that made his mouth water and his fingertips twitch with the need to touch.

"Very," she answered softly, her gaze running down his body and back up to his face. She arched an eyebrow at him, and he felt the pull of attraction low in his gut. "In a wild and dangerous sort of way."

Sable turned from the pictures and he felt her focus settle completely on him. His blood began to flow faster and hotter through his body in recognition of her attention, and he tried to remember why he wasn't interested in her.

"I suppose it would be too much to ask that you're here looking for me?" she asked with a provocative smile.

His lips twitched and he shook his head. "Sorry. Seeing you here is just as much a surprise to me as it is to you."

"Damn," she grinned at him unrepentantly. "So, what brings you here?"

"A friend of mine." He nodded his head in the direction of the rest of the outdoors collection. " He told I should come and take a look at them. I was in the area so I thought I'd check them out. You?"

She held up a battered leather satchel for him to see. "Photography is a passion of mine. I come here to work in the darkroom." She glanced at the wall of photos in front of her. "Is your friend a photographer?"

"Forestry guy. Photography is a hobby of his; he almost always has a camera with him. He took some of these on his last fire." He pointed to one of the photos that featured a line crew digging a firebreak amidst smoke and flickering flames. "That's Garret in that one."

Sable stepped closer to examine the details of the photo. The black lettering that spelled out "Dougherty" on the yellow protective gear was almost distinguishable. Turning from the picture, she stood directly in front of him.

"Your little brother likes to live dangerously." She eyed him coyly. "Any chance it runs in the family?"

"Are you asking if danger is attractive to me?" His eyes dropped to her lips and he felt a tremor of lust whip through him.

"Danger." She shrugged her shoulders delicately and stepped closer, placing one hand on his chest. "Hot things? Wild things?"

"Wild things like you?" He quirked an eyebrow at her and fought the urge to back her into the corner. He wanted to show her just how wild he could be, how wild he could make her.

Christ!

His heart pounded and his blood raced through his veins to settle in his dick. He felt positively primal around her.

Lifting her eyes to his, she whispered so only he could hear her. "I'm not really a wild thing, Gage. It's just an act. But you," She shook her head slowly and licked her pouting lips. "You make me want to be bad."

His cock stirred as he remembered the feel of her straddling his lap on the football field, her tongue sliding over his bottom lip before slipping into his mouth when she'd kissed him goodbye. He remembered the taste of her, the feel of his tongue thrusting into the wet heat of her mouth and his body tensed as raw hunger filled him...the hunger to have her naked and thrashing beneath him.

Biting back the growl of want, he forced some words out.

"If you don't stop looking at me like that, I'm going to drag you off to a darkroom." Placing a finger under her chin, he tilted her face up until their eyes locked once again. "And it won't be to develop pictures."

Her eyes darkened and she inched closer to him, her scent filling his head. "Promises, promises," she whispered, her small hand patting his chest right over his pounding heart before stepping back with a wink and naughty smile.

"Be careful, Sable," he warned. "You might get more than you bargained for."

Gage watched as her eyes widened slightly and her cheeks flushed at his words. Her surprise lasted brief

seconds before a confident smile spread across her lips...
and she threw down the gauntlet.

"I can handle it if you can."

Y Y Y Y

Sable placed another glass in the dishwasher and
looked around the near empty pub. Jake sat at the bar
playing the video trivia game. Katie was wiping down the
last of her tables, and there was a couple in the back area
doing more kissing and cuddling than pool playing. It had
been a very quiet night and Sable was ready to lock up as
soon as the couple left, which would be soon or she'd
have to tell them to get a room.

With Klondike Days, a ten-day carnival that livened
up the city every July, starting the next morning, Sable
expected a few slow nights over the coming week. Even
Jim and Bruce, regulars she usually had to kick out after
last call, had left early so they'd make it for the opening
parade in the morning.

She tried to keep busy. To not dwell on the
disappointment that another night had passed with no
sign of Gage. It was Thursday night and she was forced to
acknowledge that her challenge hadn't worked any better
at getting her what, or who, she wanted than her blatant
invitations had.

Garret and his buddies had been in again Monday
night before heading back up north for another work
stint, but Gage hadn't been with them. Maybe it was for
the best. Her first instinct had warned her that he was
trouble, anyway.

"Hey! What's a guy got to do to get a drink around here?"

Sable glanced up from the glasses she was stacking as the loud voice cut through the quiet. She strolled over to the man who had just walked in. He hadn't even reached the bar when he'd yelled out his question and she tamped down her irritation at his rudeness.

"Asking nicely is a start."

She smiled to take the sting out of her words. After all, he was a customer and on a night like this a sale was a sale.

"I'll take a pint then, sugar."

She winced inwardly at the tacky endearment and poured his pint. Placing a cardboard coaster on the bar, she slid the full mug in front of him. She was close enough to smell the alcoholic fumes coming off him and made the decision right then that one beer was all he would get from her.

"Can I have anything if I ask nicely?" He leered at her cleavage.

"Depends on what you want."

Sable recognized his type immediately, and while a smile stayed plastered on her face, she knew it didn't reach her eyes. Smiling, and meaning it, had gotten harder as the week had gone on.

"I'm feeling a bit...hungry." Mr. Obnoxious winked at her.

She pretended to misunderstand his question. "Sorry, kitchen's already closed." She collected the money for the beer and went back to wiping down the glasses as they came out of the dishwasher. Out of the corner of her eye, she saw Jake's alert posture and knew he was getting into big brother mode.

"I'm not interested in eating, sugar, at least not food." His eyes crawled over her body as he laughed at his own joke. Sable shook her head at Jake when he made a move to get up, then made her way back to the obnoxious customer. She could handle this idiot by herself.

"Really?" She smiled at him innocently.

She heard the door swing open, saw movement out of the corner of her eye, but kept her focus on the man in front of her. "What else did you want to ask me for then?"

"If I asked you nicely, would you come and sit on my face?"

"Why? Is your nose bigger than your dick?" Sable tilted her head to the side and batted her eyelashes at him guilelessly as he sputtered in shock and Jake let out a loud guffaw.

Mr. Obnoxious flushed with anger at her comeback. "You bitch!"

He stood up so forcefully his stool tipped over behind him, hitting the wooden floor loudly. He braced his hands on the bar and leaned toward her menacingly.

Sable straightened her relaxed pose, wiped all emotion from her face, and looked him straight in the eye. She pulled a bill from the apron around her hips and placed it on the bar. "Here's your money back. It's time for you to leave."

"And if I don't want to leave?" He glowered at her.

Sable heard the scrape of a barstool from Jake's direction and held up her hand to stay him but didn't take her steady gaze from the customers. "I've asked you nicely to leave. Now I am telling you, you are going to leave. However you go is up to you."

He looked at her a moment longer before grabbing the money off the bar and cursing as he stormed out the door. Sable watched the repugnant idiot leave and felt her pulse slow to a normal rate. She turned back to Jake and was startled to see Gage, fire flashing from his eyes, his rigid body held in place by Jake's restraining hand.

"Hey, Sexy," Sable said and flashed a 100-watt grin at him. "About time you dropped in to see me."

Ƴ Ƴ Ƴ

Gage felt his heart thumping in his chest and tried to calm down. His hands opened and closed at his side, and he kept his jaw clenched tight to keep from saying something stupid.

"Grab a seat, Gage. Let me buy you a beer." Jake pulled him backwards until he was forced to sit, or fall down. The hand that gripped his arm, the same hand that had stopped him from leaping to Sable's defense, released him and motioned for another beer.

Sable reached into the cooler for a bottle, popped the top, and set it on the bar in front of Gage. "Here you go, Sexy."

"Thanks."

Dark tendrils of hair escaped her ponytail, brushing against her fair skin, framing her pretty face. He noticed how her blue eyes flashed with intelligence and playfulness and felt his anger at the lecherous drunk lurking below the surface.

"Having a good night, I see."

His sarcasm wasn't lost on her, but she just chuckled softly and leaned on the bar, her full lips curved into a sexy pout. "It's getting better every minute."

"You enjoy it when men talk to you like that?"

"No," she said slowly and straightened up again. "I was referring to your entrance, not his exit."

Gage knew he was behaving like an imbecile but he couldn't help himself. He was a bit out of sorts. All week he'd tried to forget about Sable and her challenge, but he couldn't seem to control his thoughts. He believed he'd outgrown the wildness of his youth and was ready to settle down. But maybe he'd been too quick to judge both her and himself.

Maybe he wasn't as settled as he'd thought, and maybe, just maybe his instincts were right, and there was more to Sable than her bad girl behavior.

Work had kept him reasonably distracted during the days, but as soon as he left the office, his mind would fill with images of her. Every night that week he'd gone into his basement, and worked his body to exhaustion with the weights there while he remembered the way she smiled, the way she laughed, and, *oh God*, the way she kissed.

When he'd stepped out of the shower earlier that night, he was still hard despite the long blast of cold water at the end. Deciding enough was enough, he'd dressed and headed to the pub instead of crawling into bed. He'd hesitated outside the door for a few minutes, unsure about what he was doing. Knowing that his instincts had never let him down before, he'd pulled open the door and walked in just in time to hear that jerk get rude with his lady.

His lady? Where had that come from?

"It's last call—do you want another beer?" Sable's voice had lost some of its warmth and he felt like a heel for giving her a hard time.

"Go ahead and close up, Sable." Jake said from beside him. "If we need another, I'll grab them."

Gage watched her walk away and wandered if staying there was the right thing to do.

"I thought you weren't interested in Sable."

"I thought so, too." He turned and looked Jake in the eye. "But I can't get her out of my head."

"What are you going to do about it? You said the other night that you weren't looking for a one-night stand or a fling. You said you'd outgrown 'sex without an emotional connection', but here you are, showing up at the pub at closing time like you're on a booty call."

Gage looked away from Jake and shook his head. He knew Jake was only trying to look out for Sable, but he was asking questions Gage wasn't sure he could answer.

"I'm not here on a 'booty call,'" he said firmly, knowing that at least was true. "I was just restless and thought I'd drop by."

"Uh-huh."

Gage was starting to get irritated at being questioned like some fifteen-year-old taking a cop's daughter to the prom. After all, Sable was the one who had been chasing him. Hell, she'd practically dared him to see her again. "What's that supposed to mean?"

"It means I saw the way you looked at her when we were playing ball, and I also saw that you were ready to beat the crap outta that guy a few minutes ago."

"Yeah, so?"

Jake looked at Gage and smiled. "She's got you hooked, buddy, and you know it. Even if you're not ready to admit it."

Chapter Five

Katie got the couple in the back to pull apart long enough to find out they didn't want any more drinks, so she cashed out. Sable looked at the men, still deep in conversation at the end of the bar, and left them alone.

She went to the back office and hurried through her closing routine. Heart pounding in her chest, she didn't bother to fluff her hair or check her make-up. She prayed that this time Gage would still be there when she was done.

Relief washed through her when she stepped out of the office and saw Gage still sitting at the bar. She was surprised to see him alone.

"Where's Jake?" she asked in the silence.

"He went upstairs. Said he had a hot date with Angelina Jolie."

Sable chuckled quietly and sashayed over to where Gage sat. "Leaving you here alone with me? I'll be sure to thank him tomorrow." Letting a slow smile tilt her lips up slightly, she stopped directly in front of him, her thighs brushing against his knees.

She looked into his handsome face and felt her pulse kick up a notch at the heat in his eyes. Her heart pounding, she placed her hands on his hard thighs and felt the muscles tense under her fingers. Leaning into him, she brushed her lips across his lightly, but pulled back before she could lose control.

"I was wondering if you were ever going to come and see me," she teased.

"I was a bit unsure of that myself." He laughed softly. "But I couldn't seem to stay away."

"Why would you want to?"

She felt the heat of his gaze roam over her face before their eyes met and locked. Sable sensed him struggling with something and waited anxiously for his response.

"I don't. Not anymore." He leaned in and gave her a short sizzling kiss. "I want to get to know you better."

"This is a good way to start." She leaned in for another kiss.

Their lips met and her doubts faded into nothingness, along with her surroundings. The pub, and all her stress, disappeared when she closed her eyes and drank in the taste of him. His grip on her hips tightened and he pulled her closer, into the cradle of his thighs. Her breasts swelled and her nipples hardened. The urge to rub against him like a cat in heat was too much to resist.

Her arms wrapped around his neck, her fingers tangled in his hair, and their kisses got hotter. Their tongues danced against one another and their bodies pressed closer. His hands traveled up her back, pulling her tighter against his chest. Soon they trailed around her rib cage, stopping only when his thumbs brushed the underside of her breasts.

She whimpered, her body writhing against him restlessly as the pressure built between her thighs. His erection pressed against her belly, but she wanted to feel it lower. She wanted to feel it hot and hard and naked, probing at her entrance.

Gage shifted forward on his stool and Sable rubbed eagerly against him. Their mouths ate hungrily at each other, their harsh breathing filled the room. Sable's hands left his hair and ran greedily over his body. Scratching her nails down his back, she ripped her mouth away from his to try and catch her breath.

A gasp of pleasure echoed through the room when Gage gripped her ponytail and pulled her head back sharply, exposing her vulnerable neck to his hungry lips. Shivers ran down her spine and sounds of pleasure escaped from her parted lips as he nibbled on her exposed skin.

Never one to be passive when aroused, Sable brought her hands around between them and caressed his muscled chest. She felt his hard little nipples through his shirt and ached to take them into her mouth.

Instead, she pulled against the loose grip he had on her ponytail and placed her lips firmly on his once again. "Let's get out of here," she whispered.

A deep groan rumbled up from his chest and he gripped her hips tighter—this time to push her away from him. "Yeah, let's go."

Brushing her hair back from her cheek, she quickly gathered up her purse from the floor where she'd dropped it and gripped her keys tightly in one hand. He waited outside the door while she entered her security code and locked up. His hand burned hotly into her back when he led her toward his truck.

The knowledge that she'd soon feel those hands caressing her everywhere had her body pulsing with a need stronger than any she'd ever felt before.

They didn't talk as he started the truck and pulled from the curb. She turned away from the window and studied his profile. Such a good-looking man, a man's man with his longish hair, whiskered jaw-line, and ripped body.

Her fingers itched to be tangled in his hair once more and her mouth watered as her gaze traveled over the hard chest and lean belly in the neon glow from the dashboard. She also noticed the promising size of the bulge in his crotch and squeezed her thighs together to ease the building ache the sight gave her.

"Here we are." The drive was short and he pulled over to the curb gently. He turned off the truck and the silence blanketed them.

Unable to sit still, Sable jumped out of the truck before he could open the door for her, eager to get him into her apartment and into her bed. She closed the door and turned toward her building only to stop dead in her tracks. In front of her wasn't her apartment, or even his.

In front of her was an all night diner.

She looked at Gage in confusion as he walked around the truck to her. He smiled softly and brushed a soft kiss against her cheek.

"I told you I wanted to get to know you better."

Her mind raced and she felt herself tightening up with humiliation. She'd been obvious in her pursuit of Gage, had given him an open invitation to her bedroom, yet he chose to take her to a tacky all night diner instead.

She didn't know what he was up to, but she did know she was frustrated as hell and not in the mood to play head games. Sex games maybe, but not head games.

Chapter Six

Sable flopped into the padded vinyl booth and grabbed a menu to hold in front of her.

"What can I get you guys to drink to start you off with?" the waitress asked.

"I'll have a big glass of water with lots of ice, please." She ordered before muttering, "I need to cool off."

"Just a coffee for me, please." Gage looked at Sable, her head bent forward reading the menu. She hadn't looked at him since they walked into the diner and he was a bit surprised at her shyness. "Is there something spectacular in that menu?" he teased.

"Not really," she answered, still not lifting her head. "Why?"

"Because you've kept yourself hidden behind it since we sat down." He kept his tone gentle, something inside him warning him to tread lightly.

She set the menu down and looked straight at him. Uncertainty, doubts...a hint of anger. They all lurked in her beautiful eyes, and he felt a strong urge to blurt out his own confusing thoughts.

Before he could say anything, the waitress delivered their drinks and asked if they wanted to order. He raised an eyebrow in question at Sable, but she shook her head so he sent the waitress away.

"I was just—"

"I thought that—"

They both spoke at the same time and stopped abruptly.

"Ladies first." Gage waved his hand, gesturing at Sable in reassurance.

He watched her take a deep breath and let it out slowly before speaking.

"I was just wondering what I did wrong."

"Wrong? Nothing." What she was talking about?

"Then why are we here instead of getting naked and sweaty at my place? Or even at your place. I have no objections to your place."

Gage felt laughter bubbling up inside him but knew now was not the time to let it out. The last thing he wanted was for her to think he was laughing at her, when it was the irony of the situation he found amusing. Usually it was the man who was anxious to move things to the bedroom as quickly as possible and the woman choosing to set a slower pace.

"We're here because I like you." He saw confusion mixed with impatience flash in her eyes and held up his hand before she could interrupt him. "You're a bold and beautiful woman, Sable, and I know it will be amazing when we do 'get naked and sweaty.' But I also find myself wanting to get to know you as a person."

He watched as she digested his words and felt his chest tighten with apprehension. Would she be flattered, or insulted, by what he'd said? He'd learned never to try and guess what women were thinking. Instead, he just sat there waiting for her response. He didn't have to wait long.

"Why?"

"Why?" he repeated, dumbfounded.

"Yeah, why do you want to get to know me better? I mean, I've never met a man yet that would turn down an invitation for a bit of no strings lov'n." Gage heard a hint of bitterness in her voice and wondered at it.

Her image was that of a party girl. Hell, he'd thought that's all there was to her when he'd first met her too. But it was becoming obvious that there was more to her than that, and equally obvious that few men had seen past her facade. A fact that made him determined to get beneath the surface with her.

"Then you've been meeting the wrong kind of men." He gave her a level stare. "Because something tells me that as much as you try to hide it, there's more to you than meets the eye, and I'm interested in that 'more'."

He took a sip from his coffee and watched her over the rim of the cup. He hoped she'd accept his words for what they were and stop trying to seduce him. If she said she wasn't interested in anything more than sex, he didn't think he'd have the strength to say no again. Even sitting across from him at three in the morning, with the fluorescent lights of the shabby diner glaring down on her, she was still sexy enough to make his cock twitch.

"Okay." Flashing that naughty grin of hers, she sat back in her seat, looking relaxed for the first time since they got there. She waved her open hands at him in a "bring it on" gesture. "What would you like to know?"

Gage began to question her, keeping things light and easy, sharing his preferences and opinions as they talked. He found out she didn't smoke, or drink coffee, but valiantly fought an addiction to Coca-Cola.

When he tried to steer the conversation towards family, he sensed her tighten up a bit. Knowing it was unfair to expect her to open up if he wasn't willing to do the same, he told her about his family.

Her laughter at the pranks he'd pulled on Garret brightened the atmosphere of the empty diner. He saw the compassion in her eyes when he told her about the afternoon he was pulled out of biology class and informed that his father was dead. Killed by a drunk driver.

"I was ready to hunt down that guy and kill him with my bare hands." He didn't even realize his fingers had tightened brutally. Sable reached for his hand across the table. She held it in hers and he continued to talk, as if unable to stop. "My father was a good guy. He worked hard and looked out for his family. He didn't deserve to die so young. He didn't deserve to die that way."

Sable made a soothing sound in her throat and spoke softly. "You were close then?"

"I was only fifteen; he was my idol." He sighed and went on. "Garret had just turned ten and it hit him pretty hard too. It hit us all hard. Up until then we, as a family, had never known hard times."

"You were well off?" A small crease appeared between Sable's brows.

"Not really financially," he rushed to explain better. "But as a family, yes, we were very well off. You see, my mom and dad were in love. It was more than the fact that they loved each other, but that they were still *in love* after being married for more than fifteen years. And they shared that love with my brother and me. My dad was a hard taskmaster, and my mom supported him one hundred percent, but we always knew that no matter what we did, no matter how much trouble we got into, that they would always love us.

"When my father passed away, we tried to go on like always, but it was different. I didn't realize how angry I'd become. Angry at the drunk driver that only got two years in jail, angry at the authorities for not valuing my dad's life more than that, angry at God."

He took a deep breath, shaking his head at his own behavior. "I turned into a punk. The last thing my mom needed to deal with it at the time. I started drinking and going to wild parties. I'd pick fights with anyone and everyone. Until one day, Mom locked me in the basement with her and forced me to see what I was doing to her and to Garret. That they were afraid they were going to lose me, too."

"That must have been tough."

"It was. But it was just what I needed. From that point on, I made sure that I was always there for them. As soon as I graduated high school, I got a job with the Rap Attack crews and helped Mom catch up on the financial side of things. We couldn't afford to send both me and Garret to university, and I was moving ahead in the forestry industry and loving the work, so we saved all we could and when Garret finished high school, he went straight into university. He spends his summers on the crews and wants to follow in my footsteps." He shrugged self-consciously, trying not to sound too arrogant. "And that's fine, but at least with a degree, he'll have a chance at more if he wants it."

Tired of talking about himself, he eyed Sable. "What about you? Any siblings?"

"I have an older sister and a younger brother, but none of us are close to each other, or our parents."

"Why not?"

She looked around the diner, avoiding his gaze. "We were close when we were little, but somehow we just drifted apart. Each of us left home as soon as we finished high school. My sister married right away and is happily raising two kids in Vancouver while my brother joined the army. I love them both, and I really miss my brother. I worry about him with all the stuff that's going on in the world these days."

"Do you keep in touch with him?"

"Not really. I'm never sure of how to, or even if he would like to hear from me."

"Of course he would." Gage struggled to understand a family that would deliberately disconnect from each other. He didn't know what else to say. There might have been a time when he went a bit crazy after his father's death, but he'd never willingly excluded his family from his life.

"I don't know." She shrugged. "Maybe because it's been so long since we talked, and when we did talk it wasn't about anything important."

He just looked at her, not saying a word.

"He hasn't tried to keep in touch with me either!"

"True." He could see her getting defensive but he didn't back down. "Did your mother ever tell you two wrongs don't make a right? You're the older sister; maybe he's just waiting for you to let him know you care. I think all the guys overseas need to know that they're there for a reason and that we appreciate the work they're doing."

Sable just shrugged again. His comments were getting to her. He knew that, so he left it alone and switched to a lighter topic.

"So what motivates *you* when you play pool?"

Her cheeks flushed, and a glint entered her eyes. He could practically see the gears changing in her head before she smiled slowly, and her gaze fell to his mouth.

"Depends on who I'm playing."

"Oh, really?" He quirked an eyebrow at her, enjoying the way his blood heated at her sassiness.

"Sure. Sometimes pride motivates me...I don't like to lose at anything." She whispered the last part as if it were a special secret. "But then again, with the right person, losing can be just as fun as winning."

The hot look in Sable's eyes dared Gage to ask how that was possible, and he couldn't resist.

"Ok, I give up. How can losing be as fun as winning?" He had ideas of his own, but wondered if hers were along the same vein.

"You'll just have to play me sometime to find out." She winked at him. "Because you'll lose when that happens."

He laughed at her cockiness, so at odds with the uncertain woman he'd sat down with a few hours earlier. He glanced at his watch in surprise. It was 5 a.m.—almost three hours had passed. He'd be lucky to get a few hours sleep before his shift started at 8:30.

"I hate to end this, but I have to get going. Some of us have to work in the morning." He smiled sardonically, reaching for his wallet.

He tossed some money on the table for their drinks, and they headed out. She glanced at the tip he'd left and smiled her approval, making him feel ten feet tall and bulletproof. They joked back and forth, conversation flowing easily during the short drive to her place. He was almost sad to have the night end.

The sky was starting to lighten up a bit and although he felt wide-awake now, he knew it was going to be a long day at work. He turned the truck off and reached for the door handle only to be stopped by Sable's voice.

"Coming in?"

He turned to her and saw a small smile on her lips, one eyebrow raised in question.

"No," he said. "I was going to walk you to your door, like any gentleman would."

"Ya know, when I first saw you, 'gentleman' wasn't the word that came to mind."

He chuckled. "You, of all people, should know that looks can be deceiving."

"True," she said, a speculative gleam appearing in her eyes. "But I'm confident I can cross the street on my own without too much trouble. However, if you feel the need to make sure, you're welcome to stay here and watch me walk away."

She winked at him flirtatiously and opened the door. She was about to hop out when he reached across the console and touched her lightly on the arm. Anything more than a light touch and he wasn't sure he could stop himself from following her into her apartment.

"I doubt I'll make it into the pub tonight to see you, but I'll try to drop by on Saturday night, ok?"

She glanced over at him, her pleasure obvious. "I'd really like that."

She waved at him as she passed in front of the truck and started across the street. Without stopping to think, he unrolled his window and called out to her. When she turned back questioningly, he motioned for her to come to his window.

A lightening bolt of lust rushed through him while he watched her walk toward him. Giving into his caveman instincts, he reached out, cupped the back of her head, and pulled her forward until their lips met.

He groaned quietly as satisfaction rolled over him at the feel of her soft lips against his. Pulling back before he got too carried away, he felt his heart kick in his chest. He didn't want to let her go.

"I just wanted to wish you sweet dreams," he murmured, trying to cover up his shock at his own feelings.

"Thanks." She licked her lips, as if still tasting him, and turned back to her building. He watched her hips wiggle and her hair sway, trying to ignore the swelling in his jeans. He waited until she was safely inside the building before pulling away from the curb. How the hell was he going to get any sleep when all he could think about was her?

Sweet dreams, my ass. More like wet dreams.

Chapter Seven

Sable did indeed have sweet dreams that night. She woke up in a great mood and still had a silly grin plastered across her face when she joined Miranda on the Zodiac's patio for a late lunch before doing the liquor order.

"What's with you?" Miranda groused when Sable sat down across from her.

Her eyebrows rose at Miranda's grouchiness. "Nothing, why?"

"You're grinning like an idiot, that's all."

"I had a good dream last night." *A few good dreams actually.* "It puts me in a good mood when I wake up with a smile on my face. Speaking of which, who pissed in your cornflakes this morning?"

Miranda shot her a dirty look and told her to forget it. Sable sat back, got comfortable in the plastic chair, and waited for Miranda to give in and tell her what was going on. She was stubborn, and they both knew she could out wait Miranda.

"It's Jake," Miranda finally blurted out in the silence.

"What about Jake?" Was there something going on there that she'd missed?

"He's driving me nuts! He keeps dropping in to my office at odd times in the afternoon. He always has a valid reason, usually something about the food orders or the kitchen equipment, but it's driving me nuts."

"Why? I mean...isn't it a good thing that he's going to you with everything? That means he respects the fact that the pub is yours, and even though he runs the kitchen, you're still the boss."

"Yeah, I guess. It's just that I don't know what he's thinking and it weirds me out."

Sable looked at her friend closely. Jake and Miranda? She'd never have thought Jake was Miranda's type, or visa versa, but stranger things had been known to happen.

"Don't be so hard on yourself. Running a pub is a lot different that being a legal secretary. Give yourself some time to get comfortable." Sable gave her an encouraging smile. "In little more than a month, you've picked up the administrative stuff easily. You have no problems with the payroll or the bookkeeping, and after today, you'll be doing the liquor order on your own as well. The next big step is learning the kitchen aspect of the business. You told Jake you'd be working a few shifts with him some time soon, right?"

"I mentioned it."

"Maybe he's just trying to ease you in a little bit at a time. Don't worry, soon you'll be demanding everyone call you Boss Lady instead of Miranda and feel justified in doing so."

She joked around some more until Miranda seemed to loosen up. Sable knew her family was giving her a hard time about keeping the pub instead of selling it, but Sable thought it was the right decision and intended to stick by her friend.

Lunch passed quickly after that. They shared salad and chicken wings while gossiping about clothes, hairstyles, and the great weather they were finally getting. When the plates had been removed from the table, Mandy sat back and studied her.

"Ok. Your turn."

"My turn?" Sable tried to look innocent. Part of her knew it was a lost cause. Mandy knew her too well, but she tried anyway.

"What's on your mind? Don't try to deny it. I know something is going on. You're talking a mile a minute about nonsensical things, and that's just not your style."

Sable shrugged, trying to act nonchalant. "Gage dropped in last night."

"And?"

"And I made another pass at him, this one not so subtle." She grimaced. "I thought we'd finally reached an understanding. We were going at it so hot and heavy there for a while that I wasn't sure we were going to make it out of the pub. When he said 'Let's go,' I thought we were going to my place, but he took me to a diner!"

"Maybe he was hungry?"

Sable glared at Miranda's snicker. She wasn't going for laughs with this story.

"Oh, he was hungry all right," she said. "I could feel how hungry he was pressed up against my belly. And what he was hungry for wasn't on the menu at the diner."

She paused. She was almost scared to voice her thoughts. If she admitted what her feelings were, they'd be real. If they were real, she could get hurt.

"Sable?" Mandy's voice was soft, gentle.

Never one to back down from anything, Sable spilled her guts.

"The thing is, at the diner he said he wanted to get to know me, and he asked all these questions about my family and what I like to do. He told me some really personal stuff about himself and...he really made me like him, Mandy."

"That doesn't have to be a bad thing."

"I get that. In theory anyway, but experience has taught me different. Every time I've started to think a guy liked me for me, I've gotten hurt. We both know I'm not good at relationships, and that's just what Gage is looking for."

Miranda's eyes gentled, love and compassion softening her features. "Just because you made some bad choices before about who to have a relationship with doesn't mean you're bad at relationships. Everybody makes bad choices; that's how we learn from our mistakes."

"It's not just men though, Mandy. What about my family? You know I barely see them, and when we do get together, they drive me batty! I haven't met anyone that I can spend a lot of time with and not go crazy." She ran a tense hand through her hair before shaking her head slowly. "Why am I even considering this? I'm not. I'm not considering it. Relationships just aren't for me. I'll just have to forget about Gage and find another stud to entertain me while I'm in town."

"We have a good relationship."

The words were even more effective in their quietness.

She looked at Miranda and felt her chest tighten. Miranda was right. They did have a relationship. A good, strong, lifelong one that came about simply because Miranda had never given up on her. Even when she'd pushed her away or told her to back off, or when she left on her overseas trips for months at a time. Miranda had never failed to write or email her to keep in touch. Her perseverance was why they were still friends. After twelve years, Sable had come to the conclusion that Miranda was never going to let her walk out of her life and had accepted her with open arms, and an open heart.

Miranda looked directly in her eyes and spoke firmly. "I liked Gage, and I think you should give him a chance. The fact that he wants to take things slow means he's interested in more than just a roll between the sheets."

"I know," Sable sighed and gave her friend a shaky smile. "What really scares me is...he's making me want more than that, too."

Chapter Eight

Sable knew she looked good as she did a light spin in front of the mirror. Wrapped around her hips was a midnight blue sarong, shot through with lighter shades that showed when she moved. The tight tank top she chose to wear with it matched one of the lighter shades of blue in the skirt and made her feel sexy and daring. Baring a couple of inches of smooth skin between her sarong and the edge of the top, it hugged her rib cage lovingly and cupped her full breasts firmly. There was no need to wear a bra, so she chose to go without.

Last night, Gage had stopped in the pub as promised, but he hadn't stuck around. After grabbing a bite to eat, he'd asked her to go to Klondike Days with him on Sunday, her day off.

Trying hard not to stammer and stutter, she'd agreed to the date and climbed onto the cloud that had carried her through the rest of the night. He'd asked her out on a date. A real honest-to-God date!

It was now noon on Sunday and Gage was due at any minute.

She stood still, checked out the image in the mirror, and tried to decide if she was overdressed for a date at the fairgrounds.

She'd let her chestnut hair dry naturally and it framed her face, hanging past her shoulders in gentle waves. In theme with the natural hair, she kept her make-up minimal—pale eye shadow, dark mascara, and her trademark scarlet lipstick.

She knew her hair would whip around when they went on rides if she left it down, but she was willing to deal so she could look good for Gage. She wanted him panting after her by the time they got back to her door. She was aiming to get him inside this time.

The doorbell rang, and her heart jumped in her chest. She dashed over to the wall panel and pressed the button to let him in. He was right on time.

He was also breathtaking. She stood at the top of the stairs outside her door and watched him come closer with every step, and tried to calm her beating heart.

Dressed in a pair of snug, worn jeans that emphasized the muscles in his thighs and a black T-shirt that stretched tight across his chest, he looked like the type of guy only a crazy person would want to meet in a dark alley.

Call me crazy.

She sucked her bottom lip between her teeth and hoped her thoughts weren't *too* obvious.

"Hi there," he said quietly when he reached the landing and stood next to her.

Sable felt an unusual shyness creeping up on her and tamped it down. Hard.

"Hey, Sexy." She winked at him flirtatiously. "Ready to show a girl a good time?"

Desire flared in his dark eyes and a slow crooked smile inched across his face. She felt the heat of that smile work its way to her toes, hitting every pleasure point on the way.

"Oh yeah. The question is...are you?" He cocked an eyebrow at her.

Sable forced a cocky grin to her lips. "I'm always ready." *Especially around you*, she thought, mentally fanning herself.

She quickly stepped back into her apartment, eyed her camera briefly, but grabbed only the small pouch she'd stuffed some money and I.D into. Pulling the door closed behind her, she tucked the keys into the pouch and pulled the strap over her head so the strap went across her body.

Gage rested his hand on the bare skin at the small of her back and guided her down the stairs and out the door. Like the gentleman she never let him be last time, he led her to the passenger door, opened it, and waited while she got settled.

Her stomach clenched with nervousness at the way things were going. She hadn't been on a real date since college and Gage's attitude and behavior made it obvious he thought of this as a first date.

"Beautiful weather for a day at the exhibition grounds," he said as he climbed into the truck and Sable nodded, unsure of how to respond. It was a sunny day with clear blue skies and a slight breeze that made the heat tolerable, even pleasant.

As if she cared about the weather. Her mind was definitely on a different level.

Gage steered the truck onto the road and continued to make small talk. He asked about her weekend at work, and she told him a silly story about one of the regulars bringing in his kid for his first Father/Son evening at the pub. When she turned the question back on him, he told her he'd been doing surveillance the night before.

"Surveillance?" she asked. "Like cops do?"

"Yup. Just sitting in my truck drinking coffee and waiting for something to happen."

"Something like what?"

He glanced over at her as if trying to decide if she was really interested or just being polite. "You really want to know?"

"Yes, now tell me about it. I mean, you said you were an environmental investigator, but I didn't realize that you did that sort of thing."

"What do you think investigators do?" He smiled crookedly at her.

"I don't know! I didn't really think about it." She laughed at herself. "Are you going to tell me more or not?"

"Sure. What do you want to know?"

"What do you surveil when you're doing surveillance? I mean, do you watch the trees grow? Or sit and count the fish in the streams or what?"

Gage laughed at her flippancy. He couldn't take offense at her lack of knowledge about his job. Lots of people took advantage of the environment and didn't know how much was going on around them, or how badly it needed to be protected.

"There's more to the environment than trees and wildlife, Sable. One of the cases I'm working on right now has to do with illegal dumping of hazardous waste materials. That's where the surveillance comes in. Someone tipped us off and we traced it back to the company that used the materials. After questioning the employees, we found that they'd hired another company, we believe in good faith, to dump their materials for them."

"The new company has agreed to work with us to try and nail the other company by calling in another dump order. Now we're just sitting on that waste removal company, waiting to catch them in the act."

"How did you trace the barrel to them?"

"Sometimes it's easy. This time the barrels had registration numbers on them and we traced them to the user company. If there's no number then we try to find witnesses that might've seen a strange truck in the area late at night. We can usually analyze the contents of the container and find out which companies in the area use those materials, and then we question them too. Sometimes it can be a slow tedious process, but I like what we do."

"What happens when you figure out who's responsible? Do they go to jail?" She was impressed with the diligence it took to get to the bottom of who did what. Gage had to be a pretty determined guy to stick it out through all the boring stuff to get the bad guy.

I wonder if he's always that determined to get what, or who, he wants. A shiver skipped down her spine at the thought.

"Not always. It depends on if we can prove the user company had knowledge that their materials were being dumped illegally or if it was just the dumping company doing it on their own. Sometimes they just get big fines. That's why we try to catch them in the act."

They reached the area surrounding Northlands Park, where Klondike Days was held every year, and parked in a lot only a block from the gates. Gage rolled down his window and paid the parking attendant before pulling into a tight spot between a van and a compact car.

"Do you arrest them? Or do you call the police to do it?"

Gage climbed out of the truck without answering. Sable jumped out to meet him before he could open her door for her and met him at the rear of the truck. She was eager to hear his answer and didn't care to sit and pretend to be a lady waiting for her gentleman friend to open the door for her. It was enough to know that he *would* do it if she gave him the chance.

"Yes, we arrest them ourselves." He grinned at her. "My department does the leg work. Why would we deny ourselves the score? If we think there's going to be a problem, we'll have local authorities stand by, but it's not usually a big scene."

"Do you have a badge?" she asked with a grin.

"Yup."

They were standing only inches apart and Sable could feel more heat radiating off him than anything the sun was putting out. Looking into his eyes, she trailed her fingertip across his chest teasingly. "Do you have handcuffs?"

His chest shook as he laughed softly. Shaking his head, he threw his arm around her shoulders and hugged her tight to his body.

"No, you naughty girl, I don't have handcuffs."

She laughed with him as they joined the steady stream of people walking down 118th Ave. towards the park. Gage's arm stayed slung across her shoulders, cradling her to his side. After a few steps, he leaned his head down close and whispered in her ear, sending a shock of lust straight through her.

"I think I might invest in a pair just for you, though."

Speechless at the mental image of herself naked, restrained, and at the mercy of this dynamic man, she looked straight ahead as they walked. After taking a moment to catch her breath, she glanced up and replied solemnly, "I think that's a very good idea."

They laughed together, and Sable felt her heart flutter briefly in her chest. They continued on, walking side by side in companionable silence. Sable looked around her at the people on the street. There were parents trying to corral energetic youngsters, teenagers dressed in various degrees of casual, all trying to look relaxed and unimpressed by the palpable air of excitement surrounding them.

She could hear the soft sounds of a guitar being played over the laughter and talking and spotted a man leaning against the cement wall of the underpass just before the gates they were heading for. He looked to be in his mid-twenties with jeans, T-shirt, and baseball cap on backwards. One foot was propped against the wall behind him, an acoustic guitar held confidently on his thigh. His head was bent forward slightly as he lovingly strummed and sang softly to the passers-by.

Subtly reaching into the pouch at her hip, Sable pulled a crumpled bill out. When they were close enough to the busker, she dropped the bill into the guitar case on the ground in front of him and kept walking.

Gage looked at her curiously, and she just shrugged, smiling up at him. "I'd rather give money to someone who's working for it than someone who begs. Besides, I think people should be rewarded for going after their dreams."

He hugged her tighter to his side, but remained silent.

Once inside the gates, they stood still for a minute and absorbed the atmosphere around them. People of all shapes and sizes strolled around the grounds, live music blared from the stage a hundred yards away, and the smells of greasy corn dogs and sweet candy apples filled the air.

Sable forgot her nervousness at being on a real "date" and anticipation surged through her veins.

"Where should we start?" Gage asked.

"There." She pointed to a small booth a few yards in front of them.

Ỵ Ỵ Ỵ

They stepped into the line for ride tickets, and Gage watched as she bounced on her toes, trying to contain her excitement.

"I take it you like the rides?" He chuckled at her open enthusiasm.

Startled, she looked at him. "Don't you?"

"Love 'em."

She rewarded him with a mega-watt grin for that answer, and they moved forward in the ticket line. Once at the window, he bought them passes for all the rides instead of individual tickets, and Sable knew they were going to have a blast.

They decided to start easy and went to the tilt-a-whirl. Lining up with kids and parents alike, they argued playfully about what rides were the best while they waited their turn. They climbed into the little half teacup, gripped the bar in front of them, and proceeded to fight over who had control of the ride. Being stronger than her, Gage could've easily taken control, but he enjoyed jostling against her too much to care about who was actually making the ride spin. They'd started slow, but soon their little cup was spinning and tilting faster than anyone else's.

Sable's squeals blended with his laughter as they spun about, their bodies sliding into one another while they tried to get it going faster and faster. They jumped in line at the Tornado, then the musical sleigh ride. Hopping from one ride to the next, they giggled and joked around like kids finally let loose in a toy store.

The excitement and exhilaration on Sable's face made his heart pound hard in his chest while the breathlessness of her voice, and constant contact with her delectable body, kept him half hard in his jeans.

"The Zipper! We have to go on The Zipper. Gage, it's my favorite!"

Gage looked at the ride in question and wasn't surprised it was her favorite. They stood in line once again, watching as the two-seat, enclosed cages rocked back and forth while being whipped through the air towards the sky and then down towards the ground at fast speeds.

His stomach rumbled loudly, and he laughed lightly. "I'm glad we're going to get this over with now because I don't think I could ride that after we eat."

"I'm getting hungry too." She rubbed a small hand over her belly enthusiastically. "After this, let's head for the games and food!"

"What's your favorite carnival food?" Gage asked.

"I've been waiting to have a caramel apple since last year's K-days."

"Caramel apple, huh? Not a very healthy lunch."

"Healthy schmeathly," she scoffed. "I'm going to eat all the goodies I deny myself all year long. I want a corn dog and a BBQ beef sandwich and a bag of mini donuts." She hesitated for a minute, smiled impishly at him, and continued. "Maybe two bags of mini donuts!"

He laughed with her and showed the man at the head of the line their passes. Time to get on The Zipper.

They walked to where another guy held the cage open for them and Sable climbed in first.

"Are we the last to get on for this trip?" She smiled at the young man steadying the cage.

"Yup." He smiled back at her knowingly.

Gage climbed in next to Sable and felt a sense of rightness at the way her thigh felt pressed against his in the close confines. The cage door came towards them, and the young man snapped it closed. The bar pressed them tight to the back of the seat, and Gage experienced a jolt of jealousy when he saw Sable wink at the guy standing in front of their closed cage.

"You want it?" the guy asked playfully.

Gage looked on in confusion as she answered him eagerly. "I do."

"Are you sure?" he teased as he looked over at the controller.

"I'm sure." Sable gripped the bar at her hips and wiggled her butt in her seat. Her excitement was a palpable thing.

"Ok." With a wicked grin at them both, the carnie stepped to the side of the cage and grabbed the corner of their cage.

Chapter Nine

Sable looked at Gage and saw curiosity, and something else, swirling in the depths of his dark eyes.

"Ready to spin, Sexy?" she asked him.

The young guy at the side of the cage stretched his reach up and then bent his knees quickly, putting the cage into a fast spin as the ride started to slowly ascend towards the sky.

Gage's whoop of surprise mixed with Sable's squeal of laughter as the ride picked up speed fast. Soon they were whipping around, not able to focus on the ground or the sky.

"Forward!" she commanded. They both leaned their bodies forward, and the cage rocked wildly. "Again!"

Working together, they used their body weight to get the cage spinning crazily, and the world spun by in a multitude of colors as they laughed loud and hard at the crazy ride.

The ride started to slow and they groaned in disappointment. When it stopped completely, they were at the top with a view of the fair grounds extended before them. Sable laughed breathlessly and brushed her hair out of her eyes. She glanced over at Gage only to find him looking at her instead of the view.

Suddenly she was acutely aware of how tight a fit the cage was for them. The whole side of her body burned with the heat radiating off him. She struggled to gain control over her racing heart and breathe normally. Just when she thought she might be under control, her eyes locked with his, and she was lost.

"Having fun?" he murmured.

She nodded at him, not saying a word. The cage rocked gently in the breeze as they moved one stop closer to the ground.

Her gaze roamed over his features. Breathing deeply, she inhaled his scent. Her nipples hardened, and her insides turned to liquid. Lime with a bit of musk—a blend that had her licking her lips in anticipation as his head slowly tipped towards her.

There wasn't any room for movement but they managed to lean close enough that their lips brushed softly.

Sable couldn't hold back a groan at the pleasure sweeping through her body and tried to get closer to him. Unable to shift her body closer, she let out a soft groan of frustration and nipped at his full bottom lip playfully.

Gage's hand cupped the back of her head and held her to him while his mouth opened over hers, taking control of the kiss. His tongue thrust firmly into her mouth before retreating in a rhythm that made her press her thighs together in unconscious demand.

"Ride's over, folks."

The pressure pinning her to the back of the cage released just as Gage's lips pulled away. She fought to get her bearings for a minute and noticed the young man standing by, holding the cage door open for them to step out. It was the same one that had set their cage spinning to begin with. And he now had a huge knowing grin spread across his face.

Gage already stepped out and held out his hand to her. She placed her hand in his for balance. She stepped out of the cage, letting it swing behind her, and leaned closer to the attendant.

"It was a fantastic ride, but it can't compete with his kisses." She winked at him and followed Gage to the exit.

Y Y Y Y

Gage didn't bother to try and hide his grin while he watched Sable settle her butt into the tiny chair and aim her water gun at the bull's-eye. She was determined to win him a green stuffed dragon to match the purple one he'd already won for her, and he was enjoying watching her try. Again and again.

She hunkered over and sighted down the gun. Her face was screwed up tight with concentration, and she looked so cute, he had to fight the urge to lean in and place a kiss on her puckered brow. Somehow he didn't think she would appreciate the distraction at that point in time.

"All right, everybody ready?" The carnie behind the counter called out. "Fingers on the triggers When the bell sounds, your guns will fill with water. All you have to do is keep the spray aimed on the center of the bull's-eye and watch your man race to the top. The first one to reach the top has his pick of prizes from the first level. Ready...set...GO!"

The bell sounded, the guns started spraying, and the colorful plastic men raced to the top. Gage let out a whoop of joy when the bell went off and the lights over Sable's man flashed on and off. She'd finally won. After choosing the green dragon for a prize, she stood up and sauntered over to him.

"For you, Dear Sir." She curtseyed.

Gage reached solemnly for the stuffed animal and tucked it beneath one arm. He watched as she stood up straight once again and grinned proudly at him.

"I told you I'd win you a prize! Now we have matching dragons."

They both laughed out loud, enjoying their own silliness before moving on, hand in hand. They continued to stroll along the fairway, laughing and being silly. They stopped whenever something caught their attention and satisfied all their latent childhood whims.

Conversation flowed easily and Gage realized that Sable was closer to what he had been looking for than he had thought. She was a woman who challenged his mind and fired up his body. Suddenly, a future with her didn't seem like such an impossibility.

"Hmmm, Bar-b-que." Sable hummed as she pressed against his side and wrapped both hands around his arm. He felt the softness of her breasts brushing against his ribs and tried, with difficulty, not to notice.

"Hungry again?" he asked her.

"Not again," she laughed. "Still."

They were strolling towards the BBQ shack when she stopped suddenly and pointed to a little boy to the left of them.

About five or six years old, he stood stock still in the middle of the traffic flow, looking lost and forlorn. There were no tears streaming down his face, but it was clear that panic was beginning to set in.

Sable went to kneel in front of the boy. Gage followed behind her slowly, not wanting to overwhelm the little guy.

"Where did you last see her?" Sable was asking gently when he stopped next to them.

The little boy pointed to the ring toss nearby, but didn't say a word.

"And you can't see her now?"

The little boy shook his head and Sable looked up at Gage, compassion and worry clear in her eyes. She placed her hand on the boy's shoulder and looked back at him.

"This is my friend, Gage. He's a pretty big guy—what do you say we put you on his shoulders and you see if you can see your sister from up there? I bet you can see everything from up there." She smiled encouragingly.

The boy looked up at him, eyes round with fear. "It's okay," Gage said and bent down in front of him. "I promise not to drop you."

The little boy nodded his head slowly and held out his arms trustingly. Gage picked him up and placed him on his shoulders, keeping a tight hold on the boy's legs so he felt safe.

"Can you see her?" Sable asked.

Gage turned slowly so that the boy could see in all directions. Sable stood in front of him, and people flowed around them, not even blinking at the sight of the three of them. As if they were a real family.

Suddenly the small feet kicked against his chest and the boy bounced up and down on his shoulders.

"Sara, Saraa" he cried out.

Sable looked where the boy was pointing and they saw a teenage girl come dashing through the crowd. "Michael! My God, I thought I lost you!" She reached to take him down from Gage's shoulders and hugged him tight.

"Thank you so much!" She looked at them both gratefully. "I turned away from him for one minute to play a game, and he disappeared. I was so scared. My parents would never forgive me if anything happened to him." Michael clung to his sister, arms and legs wrapped around her tightly as she patted him on the back.

She looked at them solemnly. "I would never forgive myself either. Thank you so much."

"Glad we could help," Gage said with a smile at the young girl. They said their good-byes to Michael, who didn't look like he was going to let go of his sister anytime soon, and made their way back to the food area.

Holding hands, they maneuvered into position at the end of the line for the BBQ Shack, both of them quiet after the run in with Michael and his sister. Gage glanced at Sable and noticed a tiny frown puckered between her eyebrows. Was she thinking about her own brother? About the way they'd grown apart, and maybe, just maybe thinking about tracking him down, like Michael's big sister had?

Sable stomach rumbled loudly and Gage chuckled, shrugging off his somber thoughts. He enjoyed the sight of a pink flush creeping up Sable's cheeks.

She glanced up at him and shrugged helplessly. "It's the smell! Bar-b-que has always been a weakness of mine and my stomach recognizes the scent." The air *was* thick with the scent of mesquite wood and tangy bar-b-que sauce.

Gage couldn't hold back any more. She was just too cute. He slipped his arms around her waist, bent his knees, and hugged her to him. He straightened up and felt her arms wrap around his neck as her feet left the ground.

"You amaze me," he whispered before placing a small kiss below her earlobe. He stifled the urge to run his tongue around the shell of her ear before sucking on the tiny diamond stud she wore. He felt a shiver run through her at the contact and was glad to know he affected her as strongly as she did him. He tightened his arms around her, hugging her to him briefly before setting her back on her feet.

She pulled her head away from his shoulder and looked him in the eye. "How?"

Desire lit up her blue eyes and Gage fought the impulse to throw her over his shoulder like a caveman. He wanted to carry her off and make her his in the most basic manner.

"You are so beautiful and sexy you take my breath away. Yet you still manage to surprise me with just how real and unpretentious you are."

"Thank you." She smiled and laughed softly. "I think."

"Yes, it's a compliment, Sable." He grasped her hand in his once again and shifted forward with the line. Ignoring the people around him, he curled a finger under her chin and tilted her head so she would look him in the eye. "It means that I like the real you. The one that doesn't care that her hair is getting blown all over on crazy rides or that her lipstick has worn off long ago, but does care about a man chasing his dreams on the sidewalk and a lost little boy. I like that you aren't scared to let the little kid in you out at a water-gun game or admit defeat when you can't hit the gopher on the head." He laughed softly and kissed her lightly on the lips before continuing.

"The same one that has already eaten a caramel apple and a corn dog, but isn't embarrassed when her stomach growls for a bar-b-que sandwich. You amaze me because you're finally being open about who you are and what you want, and to hell with those that get in your way."

"You know what I want right now?" she asked.

"A bar-b-que sandwich?"

She shook her head slowly and a lock of hair fell sexily over one eye. "You."

His gut tightened, and all the blood in his body rushed south at her words. He looked into her eyes, burning hot with passion, and reacted.

"You've got me." He placed a hard kiss on her waiting lips before pulling her out of the line and towards the exit gates.

Chapter Ten

The walk back to the truck was a blur for Sable. Her mind raced with the fact that she was finally going to get her hands on Gage's hard body, making it difficult to keep her heart beat at a semi-normal rate.

Silence filled the truck while Gage concentrated on getting out of the crowded parking lot and into the slow moving traffic. She turned in her seat and watched the muscles in his forearms flex as he shifted gears. Then her gaze traveled to his hands...and stayed there.

They were strong looking hands, tanned and bit rough looking with a few small scars on them. In Sable's experience, the size of a man's hands had no correlation whatsoever to the size of his penis, but if it did happen to be true in this case, she would definitely have *her* hands full.

They stopped at a red light and Sable lifted her eyes to Gage's face. He leaned his head back against the seat and turned to her. Their eyes locked and Sable felt her blood turn to molten lava at the heat lurking in his dark gaze.

Unable to resist, and not really wanting to, she shifted across the seat and kissed him. Slipping her tongue between his parted lips, she teased and tasted him until the sound of a honking horn, and a rude voice, made her pull away reluctantly.

She was pleased to note his breathing was as harsh as hers, and he now had a white-knuckle grip on the steering wheel.

"Maybe you should stay over there until we get home," he commented before swinging his gaze back to the road and shifting the truck into gear. "Or I can't guarantee we'll make it there."

Pleased with his reaction, Sable laughed softly and settled back in her seat. Unable to restrain herself, she reached over and placed her hand on his hard thigh. She looked out the window and noticed they were close to her place, not much farther to go.

"Stop it," Gage said quietly and placed his large hand over hers, putting a stop to the unconscious rubbing of her thumb back and forth over his thigh.

She sat as still and quiet as she could for the rest of the short drive. When Gage pulled up in front of Sable's apartment building, she jumped out of the truck and gave a brief prayer that she hadn't left anything embarrassing laying out in the open for him to discover.

Gage stayed a step behind her as they walked up to her building, but held out his hand for her keys when they reached the door. She handed them over with a glance into his eyes, a shiver running through her at the banked fires burning there. He had the look of a man on the edge. A thrill went through her at the knowledge that she was the one that drove him there.

When they got to the door of her apartment, Gage unlocked it and stepped aside to let her enter first. Reaching out as she passed him, she grabbed the front of his shirt and pulled him into the apartment. Closing the door sharply, she pushed him back against it and pressed her body to his.

His hands gripped her hips, pulling her tighter to him as his mouth descended on hers. Their lips parted instantly and their tongues tangled. Sable felt the hard bulge of his erection against her tummy and rubbed against him eagerly.

Her arms went around his neck and her fingers sank into his thick hair, tangling in the silky strands. Unable to stop there, her hands trailed across his shoulders and down his chest. His stomach muscles flexed as she passed over them to reach her destination.

With a forceful tug, his shirt was free, and she tunneled underneath to touch the hot flesh beneath.

It wasn't enough.

Reaching for the hem of his shirt, she dragged her lips away from his for the seconds it took to pull it over his head before pressing against him once again. Sighs and moans of pleasure and frustration filled the air as their hands roamed over each other. Gage's hand cupped a breast fully and he brushed a thumb over the rigid point at its center.

"Off," he said gruffly, reaching for the hem of her tank top.

Sable ignored him and began nibbling her way down his neck to his collarbone. The hot flesh beneath her tongue tasted slightly salty and totally manly. She bent her knees a little, placed her lips around one of his nipples, and sucked on it until it was hard beneath her tongue. Nipping it sharply with her teeth, she then soothed it gently with her tongue while her hands trailed down his firm stomach and stopped at his belt buckle.

She was so wrapped up in the feel of his muscles, the taste of his skin, she wasn't aware of his hands wrapping themselves in her hair until he gently, but firmly, tugged her head up and moved her away from him.

"I can't take much more," he said huskily. "I want to see you naked and underneath me. Fast."

Sable let her lips curve into a naughty smile and she backed away from him slowly. Toeing her sandals off, she reached for the small knot on her hip and untied it slowly. The sarong fell to the floor at her feet and she crossed her arms over her front, gripped the hem of her tank top, and pulled it slowly over her head.

Dropping it on the carpet next to her skirt, she stood and let Gage's gaze devour her near naked body for just a moment before speaking.

"Then come with me," she said, holding out her hand to him. She felt no shyness in having him walk behind her to the bedroom while covered only by a tiny black thong. If she'd had any doubts that her full figure didn't appeal to him, they were dispelled by the raw lust in his eyes when she'd peeled her clothes off.

She stopped beside her bed and turned to Gage, waiting for him to make the next move.

Y Y Y Y

Gage stood next to Sable's bed and drank in the sight before him. What good deed had he done to make the Karma Gods reward him with her?

She stood before him with shoulders back and breasts thrust out proudly, letting him look his fill. His eyes roamed from her parted lips, past her curving hips, and down her shapely legs to bright red toenails, and back up.

When he looked into her eyes once more, she put her hands on her hips and slid the remaining piece of material down her legs baring herself completely to his avid gaze.

Licking his lips in anticipation, Gage told himself to take it slow. She was special and deserved to be treated that way. He'd almost lost control earlier in the entryway. He'd been ready to take her on the floor only seconds after they walked in the apartment. He took a deep breath and forced his body to calm down.

"On the bed," he commanded.

Without hesitation, Sable perched herself on the edge of the bed, leaned back on her elbows, and grinned at him.

"Your turn to give me a show," she taunted.

Gage felt his own lips part in a smile and decided that if she wanted a show, he'd give her one.

He glanced around the room and spotted a small boom box on her dresser. He went over to it and pressed play, hoping she had something good in it. Shuffling sounds behind him made him turn to see Sable closing the drawer of her bedside table before settling back onto the bed as the mournful wail of a saxophone filled the room. Pleased to hear the sultry sounds of a blues tune issue from the small box, he kicked off his shoes and stepped back to the bed.

Stopping directly in front of her, he looked into her eyes and reached for his belt buckle. He didn't dance to the music, that wasn't his style. He just stood straight and proud, the same as she had, and let the music flow over him.

He pulled the leather belt from his pant loops and let it drop on the floor. Her eyes followed his hands back to the button at his waist and he let his hands trail over his lower abdomen for a second. Her gaze stayed glued to where he scratched lightly at the fine hairs disappearing into his waistband, and he felt his own breath catch at the hunger stamped clearly on her face.

He unsnapped his jeans and eased the zipper down slowly, a sigh escaping at the release of pressure on his swollen cock. Leaving his jeans hanging loosely on his hips, he stepped closer to the bed and reached for Sable.

He pulled her into a sitting position on the low bed, one that put her lips level with his belly button, and placed his hands on her shoulders.

Threading his hands into her hair, he swept it away from her shoulders and bent forward to nibble on her neck.

She moaned and gripped his hips in response. Her hands moved and soon she was squeezing his butt cheeks, trying to pull him closer. Not ready to give up control of the scene yet, Gage stopped his assault on her neck and reached for her hands. He pulled them from his body and held them at her sides.

"No touching until I say you can."

"But—"

He placed a finger against her lips and shushed her gently. When it was clear she wasn't going to protest, he stepped back and shucked his jeans, shorts, and socks in one swift move.

Standing before her wearing only a wicked grin, he felt her eyes skim over him as if they were her fingertips. Heat rushed through his veins and his cock bobbed against his belly, demanding he find it a warm home.

He pressed Sable back onto the mattress and lowered his body on top of hers, letting out a low moan at the pleasure of her naked skin against his. He cupped a full breast in one hand and sucked a rigid nipple into his mouth where he toyed at it with his tongue. Pulling away, he heard her moan softly and he applied himself to the other.

Sinking to his knees on the carpet next to the bed, he trailed his mouth over her soft belly and breathed in the scent of her arousal. When he kissed her left hipbone, he noticed a small tattoo for the first time.

It was a delicate picture of the winged horse Pegasus, wings poised in mid-flight. Gage traced the picture, first with his finger and then with his tongue before moving on to her inner thigh.

"Nooo," Sable moaned, her hands fluttering restlessly on the bed covers.

He lifted his head slowly. "No?"

She looked into his eyes and shook her head. "Not this time. Please. I want you up here, with me. Inside me."

Unable to deny her, he crept slowly back up onto the bed, his body brushing against her as he went.

"Now you can touch," he said before his lips descended on hers once again.

Settling himself between her thighs, he rocked his body over hers in an ancient dance that tormented them both. Her rigid nipples brushed against the hairs on his chest and her nails scratched lightly down his back to his ass. Her hands cupped his butt, and she pulled him against her demandingly.

He fought for control of his body and lost. The whimpers escaping from Sable and the wet warmth his cock was nudging against were too much to deny.

As if reading his mind, Sable reached beneath her pillow and came out clasping a foil packet. She tore it open with her teeth and pulled the latex condom out before spitting aside the package. Reaching between them, she quickly sheathed his throbbing cock.

Her hand stroked his hardness from tip to base a few times until he groaned loudly in her ear.

"Keep that up and this will be over sooner than either of us wants."

She smiled at him saucily before kissing him passionately and wrapping her legs around his hips. Keeping a tight grip on the last thread of his control, Gage slid into her welcoming body and tried not to come right then and there.

Home, he felt like he'd finally come home.

They were such a perfect fit he thought he might pass out from the pleasure of just being inside her.

Pulling his mouth away from hers, he buried his face in her neck and fought to control his emotions. Sable's body wrapped around him, fitting him better than he ever could have imagined, making him feel as if he were finally where he was meant to be.

Her inner muscles spasmed, the shock of it rippling over his cock and through to his own insides. With a groan, he lifted his head and looked into her eyes. When their gazes locked, he began to thrust slow and steady, filling her, watching all the emotions and sensations swirl about in her magnificent eyes.

Her legs gripped his hips tighter and her hands roamed over his body restlessly. "More," she whimpered, lifting her head off the mattress to kiss him.

The feel of her nails scraping lightly over his back drove him harder, his rhythm picking up speed. She was so tight, so hot, her insides sucking at him with each stroke. Fighting for control, he ripped his mouth away from hers and tried to drag breath into his lungs. She felt so good, so wild and willing in his arms that he was slipping fast toward the edge, but he didn't want to go over without her.

Her nails dug hard into his shoulders as she lifted herself off the bed and nipped at his neck and shoulders. Her teeth bit into his neck, and a long low moan of pleasure vibrated against his skin. Her insides tightened around him hungrily, and he lost control.

Thrusting deeply into her, every muscle in his body tightened and the room tilted. His whole world narrowed to the point of pleasure where their bodies met and he groaned out his release.

Y Y Y Y

"Wow." Sable let the word slip out on a hard-won breath.

"Uh-huh."

"Wow."

"You already said that." Gage levered himself up onto his elbows and gazed down at her with soft eyes and a lopsided grin that made her heart kick in her chest.

"Once wasn't enough."

"One wow? Or one..." He wiggled his hips against her and raised his eyebrows suggestively.

She laughed at the eagerness clearly stamped across his face.

"Both," she answered. "But I think I need a few minutes to recover before we start round two."

"Amen to that," he murmured in her ear before he eased off her and onto the bed, leaving one leg and one arm thrown across her body possessively.

She lay there in exhausted silence, feeling sideswiped by the emotions flooding over her. They didn't just have sex—Gage had made love to her. She couldn't pinpoint the difference, but she'd certainly *felt* it. It was unlike anything she'd ever experienced before.

Mentally giving her head a shake, she brought herself back to the present and slapped the heavy thigh lying across hers sharply.

"Ouch!" Gage said, rubbing his thigh gingerly. "What was that for?"

"That was for making me wait so long to get you here." She scowled at him in mock bad humor.

"Long?" He laughed and hugged her to him. "Technically this is our first date, Sable. That's not long."

"I don't care about technicalities." She stuck out her bottom lip in a brief pout before bursting into laughter.

She turned her head and looked into his eyes. Gage was grinning at her in such a satisfied way that she couldn't help but forgive him for making her wait.

"Okay, okay," she grumbled. "So, maybe you're worth the wait."

"Thank you."

"You're welcome. Now come over here and cuddle with me. I've finally got you naked and in my bed, so don't think you're leaving it any time soon!"

Gage shifted on the bed and pulled her into his arms. Spooning her against him, he nestled his chin in the hollow of her neck and dozed off.

Chapter Eleven

When Sable woke up a short while later, still wrapped in Gage's arms, she ignored the sense of belonging she felt and wiggled around to examine his features. He looked like a fantasy come true lying in her bed.

Her fingers itched for the weight of her camera while she studied him. She was tempted to climb out of bed and get it, but that would mean leaving the warmth she found in his arms.

With his dark hair and sculpted jaw line covered in five o'clock shadow, it wasn't surprising she'd gotten the bad boy vibe from him when he'd stepped into the pub. But now she was getting to know him better and she realized that his looks were deceiving.

Her heart swelled as she thought about how he had been nothing less than a true gentleman with her right from the beginning. Even when she'd made it clear a gentleman wasn't what she was looking for.

He treated her with a respect she wasn't used to.

Uneasy with her train of thoughts, Sable focused on the delectable male body that lay naked in front of her. Why think so hard when it could only lead down a road she'd never been down before and wasn't in any hurry to travel?

She reached out and ran her fingertips through the fine dark hairs on his chest and tweaked a flat nipple, watching as it tightened instantly.

"Insatiable, aren't you?"

A flush of heat crept up her neck and she fought a surge of shyness. Did he think she behaved like this with all the men she met? Glancing up from beneath her lashes, she saw that the eyes watching her were full of desire, and something she wasn't ready to put a name to, so she brazened it out. "Think you can handle it?"

"I'm willing to give it a try." His lips lifted in a lazy grin

"Then you'll have to catch me first!" She jumped from the bed and, with heart pounding, dashed naked from the room. Choked laughter and muffled curses sounded behind her, but she didn't stop until she came to an abrupt halt in the entrance to the bathroom. She had nowhere to run, and that didn't bother her as much as it should. Gage was right behind her, and she was quickly wrapped in his arms and hauled against his solid chest.

"Gotcha!"

Giggling like a schoolgirl, she turned in his arms and pressed her nakedness against his. "Yes, you do. Now the question is what are you going to do with me?"

"I'm gonna pretend that you didn't make that easy on me," he laughed softly and walked her backwards into the small room. "And I'm going to worship every inch of you until neither of us have any energy left."

A shiver danced down her spine at his declaration and her arms tightened around his neck. Without turning on the lights, he lifted her effortlessly into the tub and her heart fluttered in her chest. She steadied her breathing and fought the urge to stroke her fingers lovingly through his hair. Instead, she just stood there and watched, palms tingling with the urge to touch him.

He turned on the taps and adjusted the water temperature before stepping into the tub with her. He pulled the shower curtain closed behind him, flipped the lever that had the water raining down on them from above and they were engulfed in a hot and steamy semi-dark cocoon.

Pushing her newfound tender emotions to the back of her mind, she reached into the corner and came away with a sponge. She squirted shower gel onto it and, with a slightly sinister chuckle, reached for Gage.

"Whoa!" he said, putting up his hands in front of him defensively.

"What's wrong?" She blinked at him.

"What did you put on the sponge?"

"Shower gel." She looked at him and gave an unladylike snort. "I never noticed that you had something against smelling good." Quite the opposite in fact, his distinctive scent was something that she'd never forget.

"I don't. But I also don't want to smell like flowers."

She held the sponge up to his nose and waited for his response.

"Hmmm, that's nice stuff. Smells like the ocean or something."

They laughed together and Sable raised her eyebrows at the hands he still held out in front of him.

Spreading them out to the side, he nodded regally. "You may wash me now."

Her breath caught in her throat and her pulse raced at the sight of him standing before her in the dim light, magnificently naked with open arms and a devilish grin plastered across his face.

He's trouble all right!

She let out a low growl of appreciation and started rubbing the sponge over his chest in small circular motions. His flat nipples hardened and poked through the suds the sponge left behind, making her lips part with the need to lick and nibble her way down his body. Trying to maintain some semblance of restraint, she forced her hands to travel slowly up to his shoulders and then back down his chest and under his arms.

Her breasts brushed against his chest as their eyes locked and she ran the sponge over his backside. Gage leaned his head down and placed his lips softly against hers, only to have her pull back teasingly.

"Uh-uh," she taunted. "Not until we're both so clean we squeak."

Gage let out a snicker and wrapped his arms around her once again. "You think you're running this show?"

"I'm the one with the sponge."

"I'm the one that caught you and put you in here." He reached for her hands and they wrestled for the sponge in slippery space. "Ah ha!" he declared and held the sponge over his head in triumph. "I'm the one in charge now."

She hooted at his antics and made a grab for the sponge.

"Uh-uh." He slapped her hands away playfully and ducked to the left, letting the spray of the shower hit her full in the face. "You're the one that made the person with the sponge the person in charge. You can't change the rules of the game now."

She sputtered and stepped back in mock defeat. Shaking wet tendrils of hair out of her eyes, she smiled sassily at him. "Ok then, Big Boy. What's next?"

A shiver ran down her spine and her insides turned to liquid fire at the look in his eyes when Gage gestured to the tile wall and commanded her to "assume the position."

She faced the tiles and placed her palms on the slick surface, spreading her feet apart. She watched over her shoulder as Gage soaped up the sponge.

Before doing anything else, he gathered her hair up and placed it over her shoulder. When her back was bared completely to him, he rubbed the sponge teasingly from her shoulders to her hips, leaving a trail of tingling flesh in his wake. Hand over hand, he stroked the sponge and his empty hand over skin. She purred, arching her back like a cat being stroked by its master.

"You like that?" he asked softly.

"Hmmm." Unable to form words, she hummed her pleasure and rested her forehead against the smooth tile. Her mind was relaxed, but her body was awake and begging for attention.

"You like to be touched, don't you?"

Only by you. Biting down on her bottom lip, she managed to keep her instinctive response quiet. Instead, she just nodded her head.

"I'm going to touch you all over."

A soft moan escaped as her nipples tightened to an almost painful hardness and her knees softened at his declaration.

"And all I want you to do is stand still. Do you think you can do that for me?"

Taking a deep breath, she forced some words out into the steam. "If you can touch me all over without losing control, I can stand still for you." She knew it was like waving a red flag in front of a bull, but she couldn't resist.

Gage stopped stroking her back and placed his hands on the tile wall next to hers. Leaning his body in until his front brushed temptingly against her back, he whispered in her ear. "Really? Would you care to bet on that, sexy lady?"

Turning her head, she could see the evil glint in his dark eyes and a ripple of excitement whipped through her. He seemed to know she needed to keep things light. "Name your prize."

Chuckling softly, Gage rested his chin on her shoulder and thought for a moment.

"If you move before I lose it, you have to perform a striptease dance for me. *And...*" he continued before she could interrupt. "You'll have to give it to me whenever and wherever I ask for it."

Sable felt a thrill at the conditions. She was also shocked to realize that she trusted him enough to accept a bet like that. Not that it mattered, because she intended to win.

"All right. And if you lose control before I move from this position, I get to tie you up and play until I can't play any more."

"Deal."

Chapter Twelve

Gage nipped sharply at her shoulder before pushing away from the wall to resume his stroking. It only took a minute or two before Sable arched her back into his strokes, and her soft moans echoed on the enclosed space.

"You like this on your back, hmm? Close your eyes and imagine how it's going to feel all over. The soap's making your skin so slick and smooth my hand just glides across it. No friction at all."

His hands slid lower on the next stroke, brushing over her butt lightly before starting at the top again. She sucked in her breath at the tease and decided it was time to fight back.

Without moving her hands or feet, she shifted her weight so that her bottom thrust out rudely. She brushed against Gage's growing erection and the rhythm of his strokes stalled. A surge of power flowed through her at his hesitation. Just because she was the one unable to move, didn't mean she was without her own weapons.

Soon Gage's strokes stopped completely and he switched to a circular movement. One that focused on her backside and made her stomach tighten with awareness.

"Oh, yes," she moaned softly.

"You have a fabulous ass, lady," he taunted as he stroked his hands over her rounded cheeks. "I noticed it that first night in the pub. Your jeans were tight and stretched nicely over your plump cheeks. You know what I thought when I watched you bending over to get me another beer?"

"Uh-uh."

"I thought 'Now there's an ass made for spanking.'"

Smack!

His hand landed solidly on her left butt cheek and a surprised yelp leapt from her throat. Before she could recover enough to say anything, his hand landed solidly again. This time on the other cheek.

"What are you doing?" she asked in a raspy voice, fighting to keep still, to hold her position.

"You have teased me something fierce ever since I met you. I'm just returning the favor. Don't you like it?"

The sponge had disappeared and his hand had found a nice rhythm of slap, rub and lift, slap, rub and lift. Unable to believe it herself, Sable found that her body was enjoying it. Her ass was heating up, the rub after each slap teased all the nerve endings and shot needles of pleasure to her core.

"I do." Her voice was husky with arousal and she was amazed, yet again, by not caring. Her pussy was plump and full, an ache that she knew would soon be soothed.

Gage was obviously having fun with the situation, and strangely, she didn't feel any self-consciousness in showing her own lusty enjoyment of it.

As his hand continued to lift and fall on her butt there was no denying the pleasure they were both getting out of it. His voice, when his lips brushed against her earlobe as he whispered in her ear, was rough with desire. "I love your body, so soft and round in all the right places. The way a woman's body should be, soft to a man's hard."

She sucked in a sharp breath when his cock brushed against her thigh, showing her just how hard he was.

Then the spanking stopped and Gage's hands were once again stroking her body. He shifted closer behind her and his cock brushed against her sensitized backside, making her insides twitch with the hunger to feel it inside her. His breath rasped in her ear as he leaned forward, his hands going around her body to knead her soft belly. She felt a rush of wetness between her thighs that had nothing to do with the shower spray and everything to do with Gage's hands priming her body.

More whimpers escaped her parted lips and echoed in the dim bathroom as his hands cupped her heavy breasts and plucked at her rigid nipples. He pressed his hips against her, his hardness nudging its way between her rounded cheeks.

Her hands clenched into fists and her hips jerked in answer to his silent demand. She threw her head back and let out a low growl of frustration at the need building inside of her. Gage's mouth was on her slick skin, kissing and nibbling his way to her shoulder, across the back of her neck. He nipped her earlobe sharply before pulling it into his mouth and sucking lightly at it. He tongued her stud earring at the same time one of his hands reached between her thighs and homed in on the stiff little nub begging for attention.

"Ooh," she moaned and her hips pumped against his agile fingers. She was on fire, and only the man that started it could put it out.

She whimpered and moaned shamelessly as he teased her nipple with one hand and her clit with the other. His hard cock nestled in tight between her butt cheeks and she ached for it to fill her emptiness. His breath rasped harshly in her ear and his chest pressed heavily against her back. Hairy thighs rubbed against her smooth ones and she couldn't think past the roaring in her ears, the need clawing the inside of her belly.

"More, Gage," she begged brazenly. "Please, I need you."

Giving up her position, she spread her feet wider, arched her back, and thrust her ass out. One firm hand clutched her hip and the head of his cock rubbed between her swollen lips teasingly for a brief second before entering her with one swift move.

Their matching groans of satisfaction mingled in the steamy room and Gage's head dropped onto her shoulder. His lips pressed against her hot skin for a moment before he nipped her with sharp teeth and began a fast and hard tempo that had them both gasping for breath. Her tummy tightened and her insides followed. But she didn't want to come, not alone.

Bracing her hands firmly on the tile, she pushed back against him and cried out in gratification at the deeper penetration. Twisting her head around, she looked for

Gage and caught his eye. As if he knew what she was feeling, he leaned in—his chest cushioning her back, his chin on her shoulder—and placed his open mouth against her cheek.

With his hot breath panting against her skin, he slid one hand from her hips to between her thighs, and tapped her clit, sending them both over the edge. Her scream of pleasure and his guttural groan of satisfaction echoed in the small space.

When she came back to herself, she was still braced against the tile wall with Gage draped over her back, his arms holding her tight to him. He straightened up, taking her with him, and turned so that the lukewarm water washed over her. With a firm finger under her chin, he tilted her face to his and placed a soft kiss on her lips before reaching for the shampoo bottle.

Neither spoke as he washed and rinsed her hair and then his own before turning the taps off and stepping out of the tub. Emotions roiled around inside her when he offered his hand to help her out. Still the gentleman.

Sex in the shower was supposed to be just that, sex. So why did it feel like he had just made very thorough love to her? She stood in front of him, naked and dripping, while he pulled a big bath towel off the hook behind the door and dried her off before running the towel over his own body.

When they were dry, he turned to her and she looked deep into his dark unfathomable eyes. As if sensing her confusion, he lowered his mouth, and with a gentle brush of his lips, gathered her in his arms and silently carried her to the bedroom.

Ỵ Ỵ Ỵ Ỵ

Sable woke up late the next morning, a smile on her face before she even cracked open her eyes. Gage had surprised her again and again during the night.

He had gently carried her out of the bathroom and into her bedroom where he joined her in the middle of the bed, with pillows plumped and covers tucked around them, for a nap. When she opened her eyes a short time later, it was to find him silently watching her, a soft expression on his face that made her breath catch in her throat.

Completely in tune with her, he lightened things up by reaching under the covers and finding out if she was ticklish, which she was.

They wrestled around in bed, laughing and mock threatening each other until, with a final huff of laughter, Gage had flopped onto his back and cried "Uncle."

Snuggling up to his side once again, Sable threw her leg over both of his and rested her head on the curve of his shoulder while her fingers ran restlessly over his chest, content.

She'd drifted off to sleep again sometime around four in the morning only to be awakened when Gage kissed her on the forehead and crawled out of bed as the sun was starting to peak over the horizon.

After a drowsy good-bye, she rolled over and snuggled back under the blankets, content in a way she didn't want to analyze.

The shrill ringing of the phone awakened her abruptly on Monday morning. Throwing back the covers, she stumbled from the bed and raced into the living room. She stubbed her toe on the corner of the coffee table and crash landed on the couch. Cursing, she gripped her injured foot in one hand and picked up the phone with the other.

"Hello?"

"Sable?" It was Miranda.

"Yeah, who else would be answering my phone?" she asked laughingly.

"I don't know. You just sounded different."

"It's the pain. I stubbed my toe when I jumped out of bed to get to the phone."

"You're just getting out of bed? It's twelve-thirty." Miranda's voice was bewildered.

"Hey! I've never been a morning person. And I had a late night last night."

"It was Sunday. What were you doing that you had a late night?"

"I have to shower, and I need caffeine. I'll come in to work early and we can eat before my shift starts. If you're a good girl, I'll tell all."

"I'm always a good girl."

Was that bitterness? Sable decided she was hearing things and said her good-byes.

Hobbling into the kitchen, she made herself some toast for breakfast. She stood at the counter and ate it while her mind drifted back to the day before.

She'd had a lot of fun with Gage at the exhibition grounds. At first she'd been nervous with him, but somehow he'd made that nervousness disappear. She didn't even know when, but she'd relaxed enough to have a blast. The rides and the games, eating all the goodies her heart desired without worrying that he'd think she was a glutton. Of course she didn't get her mini donuts, but that was okay. She got him instead.

Her heart gave a small leap of hope but she quashed it, fast. She'd had him for one night—it didn't mean anything more than that. She wiped the breadcrumbs off the counter top and headed for the shower.

Chapter Thirteen

Gage let out a tired sigh as he hauled his ass into his truck. It had been a long, hot day and he was glad it was over. He'd driven straight out to the office after stopping at his place for a quick shower and a change of clothes that morning. Then he'd spent all day trying to shake thoughts of Sable from his mind while he worked on a desk full of boring paperwork. When the call came in about a neighbor dispute over burning rubbish, he was almost happy to have to deal with it.

The sun burned hot through the windshield of his truck, and Sable and the heat they generated together filled his thoughts once more.

He hadn't been planning on sleeping with her so soon. Hell, to be honest he hadn't planned on sleeping with her at all. He'd had his mind set on finding his own Martha Stewart and wasn't going to let her distract him.

But she had.

Sable was flamboyant and outgoing and sexy as hell. He'd watched her work the bar, and the men and women sitting at it, with the ease of a snake oil salesman pitching to a group of churchgoers. They all fell for her laughter and smiles without looking any deeper. Then his radar had gone off. It had told him that there was more to Sable than the flashy good time girl she acted like. His instincts had been right all along.

Her sensual good looks had easily caught his attention. Her seductive flirting, while playing a serious game of football, had made his head spin. The tough confidence he saw in her when dealing with the obnoxious drunk surprised him. Intriguing him even more was the flash of vulnerability he'd seen a glimpse of at the diner.

It had all come together at the fair. He'd known then that he was seeing the real Sable, completely at ease with who and what she was. And she'd forced him to see that he'd been kidding himself.

How he'd resisted her for as long as he had was anyone's guess. Not that a week was a long time, but it had seemed like forever when he knew she was eager to get "naked and sweaty" with him.

He pulled up in front of the pub and parked at the curb. Sitting in the truck, he stared off into space and wondered how he was going to deal with things. Clearly Sable wasn't looking for a serious relationship, but that was what he wanted. How was he going to convince this footloose and fancy-free woman they had a chance at a future?

Shaking off his somber thoughts, he headed inside to grab a hot meal and a cold beer before going home to crash. He sidled up to the bar, sat himself down, and watched Sable fill Katie's order before she walked his way.

"Hey, Sexy," she said with a wink and a smile.

"Hi there." He looked into her pretty face and his fatigue drained away. "How are you feeling today?"

"Fantastic!" She laughed softy. "And you?"

"Much better now."

Her smile relaxed and pleasure softened her eyes. They stared at one another for a minute, and Gage felt as if the past twelve hours apart never existed. She was so beautiful his chest ached. He wanted to jump over the bar, pull her into his arms, and tell her everything he was feeling.

The sound of shattering glass brought them back to reality. Sable looked over at where Katie was depositing her empties on the end of the bar and shook her head.

"That girl. Something's on her mind tonight and it isn't work." She smiled flirtatiously "Not that my mind is full of work tonight either."

Gage felt his blood begin to heat at the look in her eye and chuckled softly. *Man, she is a handful.*

"What can I get you to drink, Sexy?"

He ordered a beer and a steak sandwich and watched her go back to work. A short while later his food arrived, and things slowed down enough that Sable could stand in front of him and chat while she worked.

Their conversation was light and easy, comfortable. They talked about movies and music, sports and working out. There was still so much about their day-to-day lives they hadn't shared.

He told Sable that he usually worked out with weights in his basement but he preferred to get out and play sports of any kind whenever he could. Sable agreed with him saying that exercising was hard enough, but just going to the gym was boring.

"Ya know they say that sex is one the best forms of exercise there is." Sable looked up from the limes she was cutting for her garnish tray and winked at him.

"You don't say?"

"It's true. But I guess the trick to staying in shape isn't the type of exercise, but the regularity of it."

"Uh-huh."

He could almost see the wheels turning in her head and knew right then, that if he wanted to have a future with her, he had to let her think it was all her idea. If she knew that was what he wanted she would run from him, instead of to him. The same way she ran from her family and the constraints of an ordinary Monday to Friday job.

He watched her shoulders rise and fall in a casual shrug before she lifted her head and smiled at him naughtily. "You think you might be interested in working out with me on a regular basis for a while? Sort of like my personal trainer?"

Bingo!

He fought to hold back his laughter and pretended to think about it. As if there was any doubt what his answer would be. "I think that would be okay. I mean, if staying in shape is that important to you, I'd like to help out any way I can."

They looked at each other for a quiet second before bursting into laughter. Gage decided to skip his workout that night and stick around. He was tired and he knew the workout would give him a bit more energy, but he wanted to hang out at the pub for a while longer and see what her world was like. Plus, he just enjoyed sitting at the bar and watching her work her magic.

Y Y Y Y

Warmth flowed through Sable's body, hardening her nipples and liquefying her knees. She felt Gage's gaze on her as she topped off the last of Katie's drink order and forced herself to focus on the girl in front of her. She'd been lagging behind all night and Sable decided it was time to get to the bottom of whatever was going on.

Placing the last of the drinks on Katie's tray, she motioned the young girl to come around the bar.

"Talk." Sable commanded when the girl was in front of her.

Katie stood there, wringing her hands nervously and looking like she was going to burst into tears at any moment.

"It's Jason," she blurted out. "The guy from last Saturday."

"What about him?"

"We went out a few times and had a great time. He was so sweet and funny...and I thought that we were getting somewhere, you know?" Katie looked up at her imploringly.

Sable nodded in understanding. She could see where this was headed already. The sweet funny guy had shown his true colors, and now Katie's heart was broken.

"What happened?" she prodded gently.

"I refused to have sex with him last night and he got really nasty. I mean, we'd only been out a couple of times and I'm not like that. I don't just sleep with any guy that comes along. And when I told him that, he laughed at me and said I shouldn't think so highly of myself, after all I'm just a waitress in a bar."

Sable watched as tears welled in the young girl's eyes. Anger at the guy's stupidity welled up and she pulled Katie to her in a hug.

"I'm so sorry he was nasty to you, honey. But you have to believe you are better than that. Waitressing is what you do, not what you are. If he isn't smart enough to know the difference then you're better off without him."

She felt Katie take a deep breath before pulling out of her arms. "But I liked him."

"I know ya did, honey." Sable watched as she straightened her shoulders and wiped angrily at her eyes.

"You're right. Waitressing is what I do, and I'm darn good at it too. At least I work! He might have a degree but he doesn't even have a job. He was just a loser anyway."

Sable smiled at the resiliency of youth and punched her on the shoulder playfully. "That's the attitude. Now get back to work or we'll both be out of a job."

She watched Katie pick up her full tray of drinks and head back out onto the floor. Turning her head, she saw Gage watching her and felt her heart skip in her chest.

Careful, girl, he may have said all the right things, but not everyone means what they say.

Considering herself brought back to earth with a thump, she threw back her shoulders, flashed him a smile, and started in his direction. Not wanting to seem too eager, she stopped along the bar to pick up a few empty glasses and listen to a customer's joke, aware that Gage watched her the whole time.

"Bored with the scenery yet?" she said when she finally stood in front of him.

"Not a chance." He chuckled. "Not only are your regulars entertaining as hell, but I get to watch you all I want. And I could never get bored with that."

"You sweet talker!" Sable waved him off and tried to fight the giddy grin that she felt creeping back onto her face. Picking up her knife from the bar, she returned to cutting her garnishes.

He's definitely trouble. And she had to accept the fact that she was fully, and truly, infatuated with him. "So what are your plans for the rest of the night?"

"Well, I think I'll stick around here for a little while since I have such good company. Then it's home to bed."

"Bed, huh?" She looked up at him with a twinkle in her eye.

"Yeah." He leaned forward on the bar, lowering his voice so only she could hear. "I was up all night with this wild and sexy woman, and as much as it pains me to admit it, she just about wore me out."

A delighted laugh escaped and she placed her elbows on the bar, leaning down so their faces were only inches apart.

Y Y Y Y

"The only thing you saw was the bottom of a whiskey bottle."

"I saw it." Pops crossed his arms over his chest petulantly, ignoring the laughter and comments of the others around him.

Sable straightened away from the bar and returned to her work after a lingering glance at Gage's lips. Shaking her head in amusement, she listened to the regulars argue about the reality of Sasquatch.

"What do you think, Sable?" Jim called out.

"About what?"

"About Sasquatch."

Sable put down her knife and looked at the three men sitting at her bar. They were an eclectic group ranging from early twenties to late sixties, and they all gazed at her expectantly.

"I think that if Sasquatch were real he would've taken one look at Pops' hairy face, fallen in love, and carried him off to live happily ever after in the mountains."

Even Pops cracked a smile amid the laughter at that comment. He stroked the six inch snow-white beard that graced his lined and wrinkled face and winked at Sable lecherously.

"How about you, sweetheart? You think you could fall in love with this face?"

Sable sashayed over to stand in front of him and leaned on the bar, flashing both her smile and her cleavage. "I think love could be a possibility," she said teasingly. "But I'm warning you. I don't believe in happily ever after."

"Hmmph!" Pops nodded to where Gage was sitting. "You think I can't compete with a young pup like him?"

Sable laughed as Gage's eyebrows rose in consternation. If he thought anything, including their quiet discussion, went unnoticed by the guys at the bar, he was in for a surprise.

She walked back to stand in front of Gage. Reaching across the bar, she grabbed him by his shirtfront and pulled until his lips were mere inches from hers. "Right now, as far as I'm concerned, no one can compete with this one." And then she kissed him.

The room filled with hoots and catcalls as Sable nibbled at Gage's bottom lip for a brief second before sealing her lips over his completely.

His mouth opened instantly and their tongues tangled as she lost herself in the kiss. Memories of their bodies wrapped around one another, heaving and sweating as they strained for completion, flashed through her mind. A low moan escaped when she pulled back to catch her breath and she wished they were anywhere but at the pub.

A few wisecracks about getting a room were heard between the catcalls and whistles from the boys at the bar. When Sable straightened up and glanced over at them, she noticed that Katie and Jake stood there as well.

A small smile played at the corners of Jake's lips but Katie didn't bother to try and hide the goofy grin plastered from ear to ear.

"All right, enough already!" Sable waved her hands at the laughing faces in a shooing motion. "Show's over—forget about it and move on."

She picked up her knife and reached for a lemon, acting as if nothing had happened when it was all she could do to keep herself from jumping over the bar and dragging Gage off to the office for a quick romp.

When things quieted down a little, and she felt like she had her pulse back under control, she glanced up only to look into his eyes. Her knees weakened, her pussy softened, and her panties dampened at the heat in his gaze.

Oh boy!

They looked at each other in silence, and for the first time in as long as she could remember, Sable cursed the fact that she worked nights. To be able to leave with Gage at that moment, to allow him to follow through with the promises she saw in his eyes, would be a taste of heaven.

Breaking their stare, Gage reached into his pocket and pulled out his wallet. "I think it's time for me to leave." His lips formed a crooked smile as he tossed some bills on the bar. "Before I jump over this bar and do something that might get us arrested."

Sable smiled naughtily. "Might be worth it if they let us keep the handcuffs."

Gage threw back his head and laughed loudly. Acting on impulse, Sable motioned him close again and whispered in his ear.

He looked at her thoughtfully for a moment before scooping up a coaster and writing his address and phone number on the back.

"Call me when you're done here so I can unlock the door."

Chapter Fourteen

The rest of the night passed in a bit of a blur. Sable couldn't shake Gage from her thoughts and that alone bothered her. She'd chatted and flirted with her customers until the last one left. Jake had brushed off a persistent blonde that had done her best to persuade him to go home with her, and then he sat silently at the bar while she finished her closing duties. When Sable came out of the office, instead of heading for the door, she walked behind the bar and pulled two beers from one of the coolers. She walked around the bar and sat down on the stool next to Jake. Opening the bottles, she set one in front of him and took a drink from the other.

"Hey there," she said by way of greeting.

"What's up?" he asked.

Sable chuckled softly. "Why does something have to be up? Maybe I just wanted to relax a little before leaving."

"We've been working together for almost two months now and you've never pulled up a seat next to me before." A smooth eyebrow rose, amusement clear in his gaze.

"Yeah, well…" She hesitated for a minute then decided to go for it. "I don't have many friends, basically Miranda is the only one, and I've decided that maybe I could use another one or two in my life." She grinned at him. "And I picked you to be one of them."

He looked at her steadily and she waited for him to laugh. Instead he gave her a small smile and nodded. "Thank you."

Sable felt herself relax and was surprised to realize she'd been nervous. Deep down she'd thought that maybe Jake would laugh at her or reject her offer of friendship. After all, he was a man, and most men weren't interested in her for friendship.

They sat in silence for a few minutes drinking their beer, neither one sure what to say next. Then, without looking at Sable, Jake said, "That was quite a show you put on behind the bar tonight."

"What show?"

Jake grinned at her. "The kiss."

"Oh!" She felt a blush creeping up her neck. "That show."

She laughed and shook her head in dismay. "I don't know what I was thinking, Jake. My God! I've never done something like that before."

"C'mon now, Sable. You just told me we were going to be friends and you expect me to believe you've never kissed a guy in a pub before?"

"Oh, I've kissed a guy in a pub before and in a bar and in a shopping mall, a restaurant, and a plenty of other public places. But I've never done it when I was working. And it's certainly never made me want to drag the guy off and screw his brains out in the office!"

Jake laughed at her openness. "Well then, it's about time some guy made you feel that way."

She let out a soft sigh, "Yes, it is about time, isn't it?" She shook her head sharply and focused on Jake. "What about you?"

"What about me?"

"You ever meet a woman that makes you want to be the caveman and drag her off by her hair?"

He took a long pull off his half empty bottle. "One or two in my life," he said when he set the bottle on the bar once again.

"Anyone recently?"

He glanced at her suspiciously, and Sable tried to look innocent.

"Why the interest?"

"No reason." Sable shrugged nonchalantly and changed the subject. She wanted to ask how he knew Miranda's Uncle Tom and why he was living above the pub and cooking for a living, when such an easygoing lifestyle seemed so at odds with his intense personality. But she couldn't bring herself to try to get that close.

They chatted for a few more minutes, both of them finishing their beers off, before she stood and thanked him for the company.

"No problem," he said and tossed his arm around her as they walked towards the door. "I don't have many friends around here either, and this better than watching Cameron Diaz run a pro football team into the ground."

She slipped her arm around his waist and returned his half hug. Physical closeness was much easier to achieve than emotional.

They stepped out onto the street and Jake waited while she locked the doors. She unlocked her bike and climbed on before he waved good night and headed around the corner to the private entrance to the suite above.

Sable pushed off and pedaled hard, her thoughts on Jake and Miranda. Miranda had her work cut out for her if she wanted more than a physical relationship with him, his walls were even higher and thicker than Sable's.

Υ Υ Υ Υ

A week later, Sable was feeling antsy. It was Wednesday, and she hadn't seen Gage since she'd left his place early Friday morning. Not that five days was a terribly long time, but he'd said he would see her soon when she'd left his bed and by her definition, *soon* was long past. How were they ever going to manage this affair when he worked days and she worked nights? She'd thought weekends would work, but there'd been a break in Gage's current investigation, and he'd been busy all weekend.

"You could switch a couple of your shifts to days if you wanted," Miranda said when Sable had whined to her about the situation earlier that night. "But I need you to stay on the nights for Fridays and Saturdays. I don't think Rose could handle the crowds on the weekends."

"I've always said I wouldn't change for a man, and that means my shifts too. I love the night shift. The customers are so different than the stuffy business crowd you get for lunches. Besides, I need my afternoons free to work on my portfolio."

"Different is a good way to describe it." A small smile graced Miranda's lips. "How are the submissions going, anyway?"

"They're going. I've got packets out to a few galleries and a travel spread going to a magazine based in Toronto." She smiled proudly at Miranda. " And different is the perfect way to describe my customers. I like them. After all, life would be sooo boring if we were all the same."

"Good for you," she said and Sable knew she was referring to the photo submissions, and not her fondness for her versatile clientele. "Now, put the boring factor aside. Wouldn't it be worth it to be able to spend more time with Gage?"

She thought about it for a moment before answering carefully. "The time with Gage would be worth it, but I don't want him to think that I'm willing to change my ways for him. I've been a bartender since I was twenty years old, and I've always worked the night owl shifts. I just don't see the point in changing my ways for a man who's only going to be part of my life for a brief time."

"Changing a shift or two around isn't 'changing your ways,'" Miranda said seriously. "And maybe if you did make the effort it wouldn't be a 'brief time.'"

"I'll think about it."

She'd been thinking about it ever since.

Word had spread of a great photography exhibit at the Chester Showroom, a gallery that was building a reputation for launching new talent. It was the perfect opportunity to ask Gage out. They could check it out on Saturday afternoon and maybe have an early dinner before her shift started.

She glanced at the clock and thought about giving him a call right then, before she lost her nerve. She paced back and forth behind the bar for a few minutes, struggling with her unusual lack of confidence. Why was it so hard for her to call him up and ask him out? They'd already agreed to an affair, and he was the one who'd said he wanted to get to know *her* as a person. The exhibit would be the perfect opportunity.

Frustrated with her dip into self-doubt, she decided to go for it. No harm, no foul, as they say in football.

Looking over the back bar, she quickly made sure everything was stocked up and the dishwasher was empty before she could second-guess herself. It was ten minutes to eleven and the crowd was thinning out. If she was quick, she could catch Gage on the phone before he went to bed.

She called Katie over and asked if she would be okay on her own for a while. Assured that she would be fine, Sable went in search of Jake and found him elbow deep in soapsuds next to the dishwasher. She told him she was going to take a little break in the office and would he please check on Katie to make she was okay.

Ignoring the curious look he gave her, Sable dashed for the back office and unlocked the door just as the phone rang.

"Zodiac Pub, Sable speaking, how can I help you?"

"Just the woman I wanted to talk to." Gage's deep voice vibrated over the lines and down Sable's spine. She dropped into the cushioned chair behind the desk and felt instantly better. He'd called *her!*

A spark of sassiness came to life inside and she smiled naughtily. "Talk to? Is that all you want to do with me?"

A moment of silence, then a soft chuckle. "I would love to do more, but unfortunately all we can do on the phone is talk."

A little voice reminded her that she'd wanted to talk to him. To ask him out and see if he really did want to get to know her as more than a bed mate, but she brushed it aside and laughed seductively. "All we can do to *each other* on the phone is talk."

Sable could almost see the light bulb go on over Gage's head when he let out a loud guffaw. "You are such a tease!"

"What can I say? I love to tease." She paused for a brief second. "And to be teased."

"Really?" Gage said in a pleased voice.

"Uh-huh."

He laughed and Sable imagined him shaking his head at her impudence. "You do realize that, while I loved every minute of you exploring my body the other night, I still want my chance at yours."

"You can have your chance at my body whenever you want it."

Languorous pleasure seeped over Sable at his words. "I hope you're prepared to be teased."

"Greedy, aren't you?" His voice dropped an octave and Sable knew she was getting to him.

"Only for certain things." She chuckled deeply. "Right now you are at the top of the list of things I hunger for."

His soft groan echoed across the phone lines. "Don't say things like that."

"Why not? I've never played head games before, Gage, and I see no reason to start now." She twirled a finger in her hair while she waited for his response.

"I don't play head games either, Sable. But when you say things like that, I want to come down there, bend you over the bar, and fuck you until you can't walk."

Wow!

Sable's whole body flushed at his words and she squeezed her thighs together. "As much as I would enjoy that, it's not quite possible at the moment."

"Too bad."

Sable's deep sigh of agreement broke the silence. *Yeah, too bad.* She sat back in her chair, closed her eyes, and let her mind fill with images of herself and Gage. "Where are you right now?"

"In the front room at my place. In my favorite overstuffed chair."

"Turn the lights down low for me. Then settle back into the chair."

She heard some rustling sounds and knew he was following her lead.

"Done," he said.

She lowered her voice and spoke softly into the phone. "I want you to imagine me standing in front of you. Our eyes are locked as I slowly peel my clothes off for you. I'm in the mood to play and you are my newest toy. But I'm not quite sure what makes my new toy tick so it's time to find out." She stopped for a moment when she heard him chuckle softly at that.

Keeping her eyes closed, she lowered her voice a bit more and continued. "I stop when I get to my bra and panties. Do you like my lacy underwear?"

"Very nice. Red is one of my favorite colors, but I like what's in them even more."

Sable smiled to hear him put a color to her panties. Good to know he was getting into this as well. Her body warmed, and her nipples hardened. Gathering her courage, she ventured on. "Using my hands, I lift my hair off my neck, arching my back and thrusting my breasts out for you. Posing for you. I can feel the heat of your eyes roaming over my body and I let my hands follow their path. My hands trail down from my neck to the swell of my breasts. Your eyes are getting darker as you watch me do this." She chuckled softly into the phone. "Wanting to tease you some more, I cup my breasts and let my fingertips flirt over the tips. My nipples harden and I know you can see the points sticking out through my bra."

A low groan came over the phone and Sable smiled devilishly. She felt wicked and sexy, and completely comfortable being naughty for Gage. It was amazing; she'd never felt this at ease with another person before.

"I'm tired of playing by myself. Will you help me?"

"Oh, yeah."

"I want you to pretend your hand is my hand. Slide it down your chest and over your belly. It should be resting over your groin now. Are you hard?"

"Uh-huh."

"Good. Now press down with the palm of your hand. I want to feel you through your jeans."

Another groan echoed over the phone line, this one a bit louder, and Sable felt her own juices flow south. She glanced at the clock; she'd been in the office for almost fifteen minutes already.

"Follow me now, Gage. I want you to touch yourself and imagine it's me. Imagine I'm undoing the snap on your jeans and slowly pulling the zipper down. I'm on my knees in front of you now and my body is leaning against you. You can feel the pressure of my breasts against your thighs. Now that I have your zipper undone, I lean forward and kiss you through your briefs. My hands travel up to your chest, under your T-shirt, combing through the fine hairs there and playing with your nipples while I keep teasing your cock through the material of your briefs."

The sound of his heavy breathing echoed over the phone line and Sable's belly tightened, her hand drifting over her stomach toward her pussy. She touched herself through her clothing, teasing. A glance at the clock told her there wasn't enough time for that, and she was surprised to realize that at this point she didn't really want to either. She'd rather make sure Gage enjoyed the experience, than physically please herself.

"Pulling away slightly, I look into your eyes while my hands reach for the waistband of your jeans and try to pull them down. You lift your hips so I can tug them off. I pull them right off and snuggle back in between your legs. I can feel the hair on your thighs brushing against my sensitive skin as my hand circles your cock."

"Ahhh," Gage practically growled into the phone line. Sable licked her lips and kept talking, too intent on the fantasy to stop.

"So hot and hard in my hand. I lick my lips as my hand strokes up and down your shaft. My thumb plays over the head and you fight not to close your eyes in pleasure. I can see the excitement in your eyes when I lean forward and you feel my breath on your bare skin."

She paused for a moment to calm her own breathing before continuing in a quite whisper. "Then I stick out my tongue and slowly lick up the underside of your cock."

A long low, groan came over the phone line. "Oh, yeah."

"You like that?"

"Very much."

"You want more?"

"Please," he pleaded quietly.

"You said the magic word." Sable took a deep breath and closed her eyes again, bringing forth the mental image of her fantasy. Her heartbeat picked up and she felt a sense of togetherness that was almost surreal. "I continue to tease you for a bit. Running my tongue up and down the underside of your cock, flicking it over the head. Licking you like a lollipop."

Another groan echoed in her ear and Sable's inner muscles clenched in eager response.

"I stop with my hand circling the base of your cock and hold you still while I take just the tip of you into my mouth. Then slowly I slide you all the way in until my nose brushes against your groin and you're filling me up."

She stopped talking, and the only sound that could be heard was the mixture of their excited breathing. Gage's deep and heavy, and hers light and fast.

"I love the feel of you in my mouth. The slightly salty taste of you, the scent of your skin, your lust. Keeping one hand on your cock, I sneak the other between your thighs and cup your heavy balls as I start to slide you in and out of my mouth. At first I start with a bit of gentle suction, relying on the feel of my lips surrounding you and my tongue running up and down the underside of your cock to keep you on the edge. But then I feel your hands creep into my hair and I know you need more. I suck a bit harder and pick up the pace. I love the feel of your hands tangling in my hair. I can feel your tension as you cup my head and try not to force me to go at your pace. You know that if you try to take over, I'll stop completely. You are my toy, and we're going to play the way I want to play."

"Don't stop," Gage pleaded. "Please."

"I don't want to stop either. You're too close to the edge. I can feel it. I can feel you swelling and getting harder as you slide in and out. My hand tightens slightly and it slides up and down in time with my lips. All of a sudden your hands tighten in my hair, and you pull my head away from your lap and up your body. I know what you want. I want it too."

Sable's hand rocked against the seam of her jeans and her belly tightened. "Straddling your body while we kiss, I reach between us, pull aside the material of my thong, and slide you inside my body. Ohhhh, you feel so good. You fill me up."

"Ahh," Gage gasped. "More, I want you to ride me. Fast and hard."

"Our lips are sealed together, our tongues mirroring our bodies, thrusting against each other. Balancing my weight on my knees, I roll my hips and begin to ride you. I can feel you thrusting deep inside me, and my clit is rubbing against you with every thrust. Oh, Gage, that's it, right there, yessss." Sable's hiss of pleasure blended with Gage's low guttural moan. "I'm coming!"

Sable lay slumped in her chair for a minute, shocked at the intensity of her own reaction and trying to catch her breath. "That was supposed to be for you, not me." She laughed, unselfconsciously. "But I got so hot thinking about really doing that to you that I couldn't help myself."

His pleased chuckle could be heard clearly. "Glad to hear I can affect you the same way you affect me, sweetheart."

The tenderness in his voice caused a tiny flare of panic that she refused to analyze. Instead, she said a quick good night and got up to leave the office. Her steps were heavy as she walked back to the bar.

She cursed herself for slipping back into the good-time girl role that came so easily to her, yet she couldn't let herself think of their affair as anything but a good time. There was a reason she'd forgotten all about asking him to go to the exhibit with her. Maybe it was for the best—keeping it on a sexual level insured she wouldn't be disappointed when he called it quits.

Υ Υ Υ Υ

Gage hung up the phone and sat in the darkened room with only his thoughts for company. He wasn't sure whose behavior surprised him more, Sable's or his own. He'd called the pub because he couldn't stop thinking about her, and he'd wanted to hear her voice. But then she'd blind-sided him with sensual images before he had a chance to say a word.

She was so unbelievably open with her sexuality that Gage was blown away. He'd never met a woman who was that up front before. She told him the way she felt and what she wanted. Even the party girls he knew in his youth had always seemed to be more into the conquest of sex with him, instead of the actual pleasure they could give or receive. Sable said she didn't play head games and he believed her. She was into him because of the heat they generated together and no other reason.

Disappointment flowed through him when he realized what that meant. That she'd gotten all she really wanted from him. She never asked him to go out with her and didn't seem to mind that he hadn't been by to see her since they'd started this affair. When he'd taken her to the diner, the only place he could think of that was safe to take her at that time of the night, she'd seemed disturbed that he preferred to chat instead of just going home with her and jumping into bed.

It all pointed to her only wanting sex and nothing more.

He remembered her saying that she'd never met a man who would turn down a night of "no strings lov'n" and felt his chest tighten. Maybe that was the problem. Or maybe she had met one that she'd wanted more with, only to have him not be able to refuse a night with another woman. That would explain why she didn't believe in happily ever after. She must've believed in it at one point only to have it turn bad.

It would also explain why she was so closemouthed about her past and kept most people at arm's length. He knew he'd seen more than she'd intended when they were at the fair. She'd been carefree and spontaneous with him, patient and gentle with the lost little boy, and his heart had opened up and welcomed her without his even knowing it.

Gage sighed and heaved his lethargic body out of the comfortable chair and headed to the bathroom to clean up before climbing into bed. Sable was the woman for him; there was no doubt about it. Now all he had to do was make her see him as more than a temporary boy toy.

Chapter Fifteen

Sable saw Miranda step out of her office and looked at the crowd in the pub. There were men and ladies in rumpled business attire, as well as big burly men in jeans and ragged looking T-shirts with cigarettes hanging out of their mouths, beer bottles gripped in tight fists. She watched Miranda skirt the pool tables and try not to stare at the skinny blond girl who was dressed skimpily so that her numerous tattoos were bared for all to see.

She was glad Mandy had agreed to cover her evening shift. It was time for her to get familiar with working behind the bar. And it was time for Sable to put more of an effort into seeing Gage.

Jim waved from his seat at the bar and she reached for a frosted beer mug. Sticking it under the tap, she smiled at him and launched into another joke, not wanting to think about why she felt the need to see more of Gage.

Sable placed the full mug in front of Jim and finished her joke while pouring another jug for Katie's table. When his laughter turned to just a smile, she walked to the end of the bar where Miranda stood with Katie.

"So I get to work with the boss tonight, huh?" Katie was smiling at Miranda, who looked a bit tense to say the least.

"I don't know if 'work with' is the proper term, Katie. I think saying that you get to train the boss tonight would be more accurate." Mandy laughed self- deprecatingly.

"Don't worry." Katie nodded her head and smiled at them confidently. "It'll be fun."

"Maybe for you," Miranda said with a slight grimace.

"Here you go, Katie." Sable placed the full jug of draft and two more frosty mugs on the tray on the bar. "And you have a joiner at table three."

Katie slid the full tray deftly off the bar and onto the palm of her hand before walking away quickly to deal with her new customer.

Sable stepped back and looked directly at her friend. "Get your butt back here and start pouring drinks, Mandy. The only way to get wet is to jump in with both feet."

She almost felt sorry for Mandy when she took a deep breath, visibly straightened her spine, and stepped behind the bar. At first, she tried to ignore the conversations going on around her and just pour drinks, but Sable wouldn't let her get away with it. She and the regulars sitting at the bar soon had Mandy relaxed and joking along with them.

"No, I'm sorry, Pops," Miranda said, shaking her head and smiling. "I don't believe in Bigfoot."

"I'm going back up to the cabin this weekend and I'm gonna get pictures for all of ya. Then you won't be laughing at me no more!" Pops drained the last of his beer and slid off his barstool. "It was nice to finally be able to chat with you, Ms. Miranda. Have a good night, everyone." He waved to the others at the bar and ambled towards the exit.

Sable smiled at the old man and turned to Miranda. "Happy hour's over. It's time for me to head out, too."

Miranda threw her arms around her in a quick hug before stepping back with a grin. "Go get him, girl! I'm glad you finally found a man you want to keep around."

Sable's pulse jumped and her stomach clenched. Is that what was going on? Did she want to keep Gage in her life? Was it more than just lust that was making her eager to see him so often?

With a weak smile at Miranda and a wave to the guys at the bar, Sable grabbed her purse and rushed out the back door of the pub. Needing some time to think, she walked the few blocks to the nearest corner store to pick up some things for her surprise visit to Gage's house.

Y Y Y Y

Gage fought to keep his breathing even, his chest rising and falling steadily as his muscles trembled and screamed in agony. Pushing his breath out sharply, he pushed against the weight across his chest and locked his elbows before guiding the heavy barbell into the brackets above him.

As he sat on the edge of the weight bench, his head dropped forward, and he concentrated on quieting his pounding heart.

He'd been doing a lot of that recently. Listening to his heart. It kept telling him that Sable was the one for him. She was the one that he had always wanted, the one that could set his heart, and his cock, on fire. The one that he could build a family with.

She might think sex was all she had to offer a man, but he knew she just hadn't met the right man. Until now. Together they could have it all. But how could he convince her of that when every time he tried to have a straight conversation with her it turned to sex, and his brain turned to mush? He hadn't even been able to talk to her on the phone last night without being sucked into a sexual fantasy that had left him breathless, and ultimately, alone.

The loud buzz of his newly installed doorbell interrupted his musings. He reached for the hand towel nearby and ran it over his face and chest briskly to wipe away the sweat from his workout. He took the stairs two at a time as he hurried to the door.

He swung the front door open and the air whooshed from his lungs, all his blood heading south.

Standing with one hip thrust out provocatively and a naughty smile stretched across luscious scarlet lips was the woman of his dreams.

Dressed in a short flirty skirt and a tight strapless thing that looked like it belonged under her clothes, she looked like a woman on a mission. God, he hoped wrapping her curvy legs around him was part of that mission because all he could see in his mind's eye was her, naked except for those four-inch heels, straddling him and riding him like the wild woman she was.

Her chestnut hair had that tousled look that made his fingers itch to sink in her curls and pull her close so he could lose himself in the taste of her, the feel of her pressed against him, the feel of coming home that only got stronger every time he sank into her welcoming body.

"Hey, Sexy," the Goddess whispered, flames of desire brightening her eyes as she looked him over from head to toe.

The lust stamped clearly on her face made him glad he worked out regularly. The heat of her gaze running over his naked chest and bare legs almost felt like hungry hands.

Jesus, no wonder he could never have a straight conversation with her. The woman was dangerous when she looked at him like that. But then again, he'd never doubted she wanted him. He just wondered for how long.

Remembering his plan to make her see him as more than a temporary boy toy, he struggled to drag his mind away from the bedroom and find a way to make this unexpected visit work in his favor.

He needed to play it cool, get her inside and comfortable. Then when it was clear she wasn't going anywhere else for the night, he'd talk to her. Tell her how he felt and make her see that what they had together was special.

Υ Υ Υ Υ

Gage stood before her wearing nothing but a pair of gray running shorts and a surprised grin. She licked her lips hungrily and took in the view.

Midnight hair slicked back from his chiseled features, and a sexy five o'clock shadow shaded his firm jaw line and framed full sensual lips. Her gaze landed on one bead of sweat and followed it as it dripped off his chin, landed on nicely muscled pecs, and got lost in the light dusting of hair that trailed down his defined abs to disappear under the waistband of his shorts.

The treasure trail.

And if she wasn't mistaken the treasure was growing bigger before her eyes.

She noticed his abdominal muscles shaking and heard the rumble of his deep chuckle at the same time. She raised her gaze to his and arched an eyebrow haughtily.

"Are you laughing at me?"

"I wouldn't dare," he said, shaking his head innocently.

"Because if you are I'm sure I can find someone else to share my goodies with."

"Your goodies?" His eyebrows rose at that and she could tell he was fighting back laughter.

She thrust out her chest and flashed him a naughty grin, knowing he would get the wrong idea. When his eyes dropped to her cleavage, she lifted her left hand and shook the cloth sack she held there, calling his attention to it.

"I come bearing gifts."

Gage leaned against the doorframe and crossed his arms over his naked chest. "Should I be scared of what's in there?"

She'd had enough teasing; it was time to get serious. Stepping close enough that she could smell the manly musk radiating off him, she placed a finger on the rapidly beating pulse at the base of his throat. She looked up into his eyes and let him see the depth of her desire for him. "Why don't you invite me in and find out?"

His dark eyes brightened and she felt the pulse under her finger jump. He looked at her with an intensity that made her heart pound in her chest and her blood turn to hot lava running through her veins. "The only way you're getting in is if you promise to stay the whole night."

A thrill shot through her and she responded without thinking. "I promise," she whispered and leaned in to kiss him.

Her lips had barely brushed his when he pulled away from her and stepped back into the entrance of the house. "Please come in then." Avoiding her eyes, he made a huge sweeping gesture with his arm.

Sable stepped into the house and stopped a few feet in, unsure of where to go. She'd been pretty confident in her seduction scheme until he'd pulled away from her kiss. Now uncertainty reared its ugly head, and she stood unsure of what to do next. Maybe she'd made a mistake, maybe he wasn't as eager to see more of her, as she was of him.

Gage walked up behind her and she felt the heat of him tease her senses. Unwilling to turn and face him, she clenched the fist holding the satchel of wine and fruit she'd brought along and tried to steady her breathing.

"This is a pleasant surprise," he said softly from directly behind her.

"After our conversation last night, I decided to take Miranda up on her offer to cover a shift for me." She answered without turning to him. "I hope you don't mind me just dropping in?"

"Not at all." He stepped beside her and grasped her hand in his. "But I need to finish my workout if that's okay with you? I only have one more set." Without waiting for an answer he led her towards the door at the end of the hallway and she followed him down the steps into the half-finished basement.

Her heels sank into the soft carpet as Gage led her towards the only piece of furniture she could sit on. A large antique looking cedar chest was set against the drywall, directly in front of the small weight bench that held a barbell with some very large and heavy looking steel plates on it.

"Are you bench pressing that?"

"Yeah." He sat on the end of the bench and smiled at her. "It's not as impressive as it looks."

"You can do more?"

"I think so, yeah. But I won't try it until Garret's home this weekend to spot me." He lay back on the bench and reached for the barbell above him.

Sable watched as his chest rose and fell, his breathing matching his smooth even repetitions. Her gaze roamed over his body in that position and her breasts swelled, her nipples hardening instantly. *God, he was beautiful.*

His whole body was lightly dusted with dark hairs that couldn't hide the way his muscles tensed and jumped with each movement. Her mouth filled with saliva, and the urge to get on her knees and lick him all over swelled inside her.

An image flashed in her brain and she felt her inner bad girl strain to get lose. Why fight it? Gage had told her he loved her lustiness. No use hiding her desire from him.

She watched as he slid the barbell home in its brackets and sat up, facing her once again. Looking into his eyes and not saying a word, she stood up slowly and closed the distance between them.

"Sable –"

"Shhhh," she whispered and pressed a finger to his lips. She watched a battle being fought briefly in his eyes before he relaxed, and sharp teeth nipped her fingertip.

Dropping her hand to her side, she smiled at him seductively, and slowly raised her skirt. Straddling him, and the bench, she settled herself on his lap. She placed her arms around his neck loosely, rested her forehead against his, and whispered, "It's time for me to work up a sweat. Lay back and enjoy the ride."

With that she placed her lips on his and began to feed the bottomless hunger she had for him. Leaning into him, she carefully pressed him back onto the cushioned bench. His hands ran over her back and held her tight to him.

Feeling his hips press into her, she rolled her hips and gasped as his growing hardness found a soft spot that sent pleasure rippling through her body. Dragging her lips away from his, she licked and nibbled at his neck, tasting him and teasing him at the same time.

She reached behind her and grasped his hands in hers. Bringing them forward, she sat up on top of him and placed his hands back on the barbell. Looking deep into his eyes, she instructed him to keep his hands there.

"You told me last night that I could have my chance at exploring your body anytime I wanted, and that's what I'm going to do." She wiggled her hips back, leaned forward, and placed her mouth against the pulse pounding at the base of his neck. Pulling back slightly, she blew warm air onto his skin and watched a small shiver rack his tight body.

Heavy breathing filled the room but neither of them spoke. Staying just barely above him, she brushed the hard tips of her breasts against his bare stomach. She looked at the darkness of her hair against his skin, the softness of her curls against the hardness of his muscles. Swinging her head slightly from side to side, she let the ends brush against his firm chest, tickling his hardening nipples.

Feeling his cock swell beneath her, she fought the urge to grind against him and stood up quickly.

"Uh-uh," she said sharply when he made to follow her. "I said no moving. Just watch and feel."

She stood beside the bench so he could see her clearly without straining and started to slowly remove her clothes before she followed through on every teasing word she'd used to get them both off the night before.

Υ Υ Υ Υ

"Do you believe in reincarnation?"

Sable sat in the middle of Gage's bed eating fruit and cheese and sipping wine from a coffee mug - the "goodies" she'd had when she'd shown up at his door. Caught by surprise, Gage looked at her closely and felt his heart swell in his chest.

Wearing one of his T-shirts that she'd pulled on after stepping out of another shared shower, with no make-up and her hair drying naturally about her shoulders, she'd never looked more beautiful to him.

"I never have before, but if you tell me you're Aphrodite reincarnate, I'll believe you."

Her mouth opened and a loud bark of laughter escaped, charming him even more.

"I'm already in your bed, Gage. You don't have to use lines on me."

"It's not a line, Sable."

"Telling me I'm a sex goddess reincarnate isn't a line?" She arched a brow at him.

"Not really. You have a lot in common with her."

"Yeah?" She shook her head and chuckled at him. "Is that a nice way of saying I'm too into sex?"

"No!" He shook his head adamantly. "Not at all. It's my way of telling you that I know you have more to offer than mind blowing sex."

"Mind blowing, huh?"

He saw her lips twitch with laughter, but he saw his opening and took it.

"Yes, mind blowing." He grinned at her, slapping at the hand that stretched toward his naked chest. "Now keep your hands to yourself while I explain what I see in you."

She sat up straight and folded her hands primly in her lap. "Please do, kind sir," she said with a twinkle in her eye.

Grinning at her silliness, he shook his head gently. "What most people don't know is that there are two Aphrodites. Some say there were two separate goddesses of love while others say it was just a split in her character." Sable had stopped eating and was watching him intently, interested in what he was saying and absorbing it.

Good, maybe she'd see the parallels clearly.

"Celestial Aphrodite is the stronger of the two, more intelligent and spiritual. This Aphrodite represents philosophy and religion and pure spiritual love. Then there's Aphrodite Pandemos that is essentially physical in nature, the goddess of physical attraction and procreation. While no one can ever say for sure if they were one and the same, I think you have all of those aspects in you." He hesitated for a moment before plunging ahead. "And I think that like her, you try very hard to keep them separate."

He watched as she chewed thoughtfully on her full bottom lip and waited to hear what she had to say. He didn't have to wait long.

"You think I'm intelligent and spiritual? That I'm a natural philosopher?"

While she was careful to keep her face blank, except for a small smile, he thought he detected hope in her eyes.

"Yes, I do, sweetheart." He reached across the empty platter between them and cupped her cheek in his hand. Her skin was so soft and warm against his fingers. "I think that you are one of the most intelligent, caring, loving and special people I have ever had the good fortune to have in my life. And I hope to keep you there for a long time to come."

He looked deep into her eyes and let all his emotions float to the surface. Sable's eyes widened, and he knew she was seeing what he felt. He saw excitement, arousal, and longing swirl in her eyes before panic set in.

The second he saw her start to pull back, he leaned across the bed and covered her lips with his. Putting all he felt into the kiss, he nibbled at her lips and seduced her tongue out of hiding the same way he had seduced her dreams out of her, with patience and openness.

Her arms slid around his neck, and he tossed the plastic container that had held the fruit and cheese onto the floor and pushed her back onto the bed, covering her body with his.

Chapter Sixteen

Sable saw Gage stride into the Zodiac and fought the urge to hide. He saw her standing by the pool tables and changed directions, heading straight for her. For the first time that night, she was glad it was dead quiet in the pub. She didn't need an audience for this conversation. Trying to keep things casual, she pasted a smile on her face and greeted him.

"Hey there! How was work today?"

He stopped directly in front of her. "It would've been better if you'd been there when I woke up, like you promised." His voice wasn't actually accusatory, but the look in his eyes made her feel pretty small.

How was she supposed to tell him that the emotion he shown her had been too much? That she'd woken up wrapped in his arms and *had* to leave?

"Sorry about that. I woke up early and couldn't get back to sleep. I didn't want to disturb you so I left around five." She shrugged, noticing Jake help himself to a coke behind the bar. He was watching her and Gage, and when he finished filling his glass, stayed behind the bar, chatting with Katie. "I spent the night. I didn't think my not being there would be such a big deal."

She saw a brief struggle going on in his eyes and then he seemed to come to a decision. "Sable, having you –"

Panic began creeping up on her when he started to speak and she interrupted him. "Gage, it wasn't a big deal."

If his steady gaze made her heart pound in her chest, his next words made it stop completely. "Sable, it is a big deal. I wanted to wake up with you still in my bed. I wanted to go to work knowing that you were still in my bed, the same way you're in my heart."

Sable started to shake her head and he reached for her hands, holding them tightly in his. "I love you, Sable, and I wanted to wake up and tell you that first thing in the morning. The same way I want to do that every morning for the rest of my life."

Sable's chest tightened and she tried desperately to breathe.

Who did he think he was, saying those things? She thought he had understood that what they had wasn't a relationship. It was an affair. Why did he have to go and get all emotional? Isn't it supposed to be the woman that gets emotional, the woman that gets hooked on dreams of happily ever after and a white picket fence?

Her blood ran hot and her heart beat a fast tattoo. This was it. It was time to cut and run. She pulled her hands out of his tender grip and stepped back. Taking a deep breath, she looked him the eyes. Those gorgeous, dark, bottomless eyes of his. "I'm sorry you feel that way, Gage."

"Why are you sorry?" He didn't seem surprised by her response, only curious.

"Because I'm no good at relationships, and I thought it was understood that this was just for fun." She dropped her eyes to the floor and tried to steady her shaking hands. Why were they shaking anyway?

"What made you think I was only in this for fun?" he asked gently.

Sable struggled to find the answer. What had made her think he was in it for fun? "All men are only looking for a good time."

"Do you remember when I took you to the diner for coffee? And you told me you'd never met a man that could turn down a night of no strings sex?"

Crossing her arms over her chest, she looked into his eyes. "I remember."

"Do you also remember what I said to that?"

She looked at him for a moment before nodding her head once.

"What did I tell you, Sable?"

"That I'd been meeting the wrong kinds of guys."

"And?"

"That you wanted to get to know me."

They looked at each other and the silence lengthened. A small smile graced Gage's lips and love welled up from the depths of his bottomless eyes. Her heart pounded, her chest tightened, and she struggled to breathe.

Dragging her eyes from his, she started to step away from him only to feel his hands settle on her shoulders. She felt funny—her chest ached and she struggled to pull air into her lungs. She had to walk, had to move, but his hands kept her there with him.

Her eyes darted wildly around the room and a roaring sound filled her ears. She shrugged her shoulders and pulled away from Gage. Her eyes met his and she felt her heart crack. "I'm sorry," she uttered before she turned and ran from the pub, leaving him standing there like a statue.

Y Y Y Y

Gage eyed the classy brunette sitting alone at the dinner table ten feet in front of him. As if she felt his gaze, she turned her head, a smile spreading across her face when she saw him.

An answering smile came easily to his lips. It was the first time in days that he felt somewhat normal. "Marcy," he said, closing the distance between them. "I'm glad you called. It's good to see you again."

He settled into the chair across from his best buddy's little sister, and ordered a much-needed scotch from the waiter.

"I didn't even know you were coming to town. How are Darren and Christa doing?"

"Good," she answered. "Everyone is good, and everything's the same. You know small towns, not much changes as time goes on. How about you?"

He shrugged, unsure how to answer that. If she'd asked him three days ago how he was, he'd have answered with a hearty "Fantastic!" but that was before

Sable had run from him. Before he'd told her he was in love with her.

It seemed his lover was afraid of love. And when she was afraid, she ran.

Frustration had been his constant companion lately, but he pushed it aside to focus on Marcy. Almost a week had passed and he hadn't seen or talked to Sable. She wouldn't return any of his calls, and he wasn't desperate enough to chase her down at work. Yet.

"Gage?" Marcy's voice cut into his thoughts.

"Sorry, Marcy." He gave his head a shake. "I drifted off for a minute there, thinking about an investigation."

"How do you like the new job?"

He didn't have to think twice before answering that one. "The new job is going good. It's certainly different than working the fire crews, but I'm enjoying it."

The waiter appeared and they ordered their meals, conversation flowing easily once they were alone again. Marcy told him about her job at the bank, a recent promotion, and he pretended to be interested, but he couldn't stop thinking about Sable. Until Marcy's words began to sink in.

"I admit, I never thought I'd hear that you were planning to settle down and all that. Yet, here you are, a stable homeowner with a safe, solid career." A predatory gleam entered her eyes when she continued. "All you need now is a good woman and you're set."

Gage chuckled and asked about the seminar she was in town for. He didn't want to think about how lousy his plans for settling down were going. Unless...

He took a good long look at the woman he was about to have dinner with and realized Darren's little sister wasn't so little anymore. He eyed the discreet amount of cleavage displayed by her button-up blouse, her sleek hairstyle, and perfect fingernails. No, she wasn't the same youthful co-ed he'd met five years ago at Darren's parents' place.

In fact, she looked exactly like the type of woman he'd pictured himself with when he made the decision to settle down. Polished, professional, but not so into her career that she wouldn't make room to raise a family.

The waiter arrived with their meals and they began to eat. Conversation remained superficial during dinner and Gage watched as Marcy picked at her grilled chicken breast and green salad. Images of Sable's laughing face as she scarfed down candy apples and corn dogs at the fair played on the screen in his head.

"I wouldn't mind living in the city," Marcy said, smiling at him seductively.

He wasn't surprised when he felt nothing at her come-on but a touch of male satisfaction. Sable had chased him until she'd caught him, body and soul, and now she wanted to walk away. Marcy was the ideal of what he'd had in mind when he'd decided to settle down. She might not make his heart pound in his chest or his dick stand at attention, but she was here. And she was making it clear she was looking for the same thing he was. Someone to settle down with.

Y Y Y Y

Sable ripped open the letter from The Globetrotter magazine and pulled out the single sheet of paper. She skimmed the letter, sank into the office chair, and read it again. Slowly.

It was a job offer. A job offer to be a staff photographer at their Toronto office. She'd sent them some of her scenery pictures from South Africa, hoping for a sale. She'd never expected a job offer. She instinctively reached for the phone, only to remember that she couldn't call Gage. She'd stopped seeing him.

Miranda strode into the office and stopped dead, staring at her. "Sable? What is it?"

She looked into Miranda's face and saw concern in the pucker of her brow. She waved the letter at her weakly. "It's a job offer from a magazine in Toronto."

Miranda sat in the chair behind the desk. "I didn't know you wanted to work for a magazine. I thought you used the commercial photography to pay for the artistic side of things."

"I do. I mean, I did." She explained to Mandy that she'd sent in some pictures to sell, and instead of just buying the pictures, the magazine had countered with a job offer.

"Are you going to take it?" she asked.

Sable shook her head. "I won't leave you, Mandy. Not until you're ready for me to go, you know that."

She saw Miranda's shoulders relax for a second and then straighten up again. "I think you've taught me all you can about this business, Sable. The rest is up to me. If you want the job, don't let me stop you from taking it."

"Really?" She'd known for a while now Mandy had a good handle on the business, that all she'd needed was some confidence, but she was surprised to discover that Mandy felt the same way.

She sat back in her chair and went over the pros and cons of the job offer with her best friend, trying to feel excited.

She knew why she wasn't eager to accept the offer, and it wasn't just because it wasn't her dream job. In fact, working as a staff photographer would be a bigger step towards her ultimate dream of her own show than working behind a bar.

It was Gage. She couldn't bear the thought of not ever seeing him again. Somehow, even though she'd told herself, and him, that they were done, she didn't feel as if it was really final. But moving to Toronto would make it final.

She stood up suddenly and grinned at Mandy. "Will you watch the bar for me for an hour?"

"Sure, why?"

"I need to go see Gage. To talk to him." Her voice was calm and sure. Not at all like her insides.

Miranda, who knew she'd stopped seeing Gage and disapproved, beamed at her and waved her away. "Take the night off. Go fix things with that man!"

Sable called a cab and headed straight to Gage's house. But when they were on the edge of Downtown she saw a distinctive yellow truck parked in front of an Italian restaurant and told the cabbie to pull over. The forestry sticker on the windshield told her it was Gage's truck, so she climbed out of the cab. He must've decided he wanted Italian for dinner.

No longer denying how much she'd missed him in the past week, Sable didn't bother to hide her monster grin as she stepped into the restaurant. She looked past the hostess and spotted Gage's midnight hair not far away. Two steps in, she noticed the woman he was with. A conservatively dressed, classically pretty brunette who had his hand clasped between both of hers.

Pain knifed through her heart and Sable gasped. Turning quickly, she stumbled out of the restaurant. Leaning against the solid brick of the building, she clutched her chest as if to hold the pain in. She didn't see the people walking by on the street, instead she saw the emotion swirling in Gage's dark eyes the last time they'd made love.

They'd made love. It was better, more intense and fulfilling, than anything she'd ever experienced. It had been the first time she'd ever felt truly loved...and she'd run from it.

Now it was too late. She'd chased him when she'd wanted an affair, and he'd turned her down. He made her believe he wanted to get to know her, to really know *her*. And once she let down her guard and let him in, he didn't care enough to chase her back.

She was right from the beginning. Men didn't want to be with her, to love her, and Gage was no different. She was only good for a good time.

Dreams she wasn't even aware she'd had disappeared into mist and her resolve hardened. How could she have been so stupid as to believe there could've been any more to it than that, no matter what he'd said? Obviously she hadn't been *that* special. He'd moved on already.

Wiping the tears from her cheeks, she straightened away from the wall, ignored the fact that the silent tears wouldn't stop flowing, and walked away.

It was time for her to move on, too.

Chapter Seventeen

Gage twisted his key in the lock and entered his empty house. Without turning on any lights, he went to the front room and sank into his favorite chair. The overstuffed one that was next to the phone stand. The one he'd sat in the night Sable had talked dirty to him while he jerked off.

Closing his eyes, he replayed the night over in his mind. Dinner had been nice, but he couldn't believe he'd actually considered dating Marcy when he was so completely in love with Sable. Marcy may have been what he'd originally wanted, but Sable was what he needed. That thought had hit him right between the eyes when Marcy had reached across the dinner table, taken his hand in hers, and made it clear that she was interested in settling down too. With him.

He'd felt a heaviness in his chest and known instinctively she was not who he wanted, no matter how perfectly she fit his original idea of what he'd been looking for.

He sighed heavily and scrubbed a hand over his face. How long would he have to wait until Sable realized that he was what she wanted? He'd give her another week, and then he was going after her.

Υ Υ Υ Υ

"Are you going to keep running forever?"

Sable glared at Mandy, but kept sticking the beer in the cooler. "I'm not running."

She'd arrived at the pub early that day, after crying herself to sleep the night before, and gave Miranda her notice. At first Miranda had accepted it with nothing more than a quizzical smile, but when Sable didn't explain anything further, she'd followed her out of the office and behind the bar. With Happy Hour still an hour away, the pub was empty except for a couple of businessmen in a booth against the far wall and Jake, who sat at the bar nursing a Coke before his shift started.

"Really? Then why are you moving to Toronto to take a job you don't want?"

"I told you, it might not be my dream job, but at least it's photography." She shrugged. "I could do worse."

"Like bartending for me?"

The hurt in Miranda's voice surprised Sable. "No! I love working here, you know I do. But..." She looked at Jake, considering. She hadn't told them about seeing Gage with another woman. It hurt too much to tell anyone. "Things have changed for me here, and I think it's time to move on. I just have itchy feet, you know that, Mandy."

Planting her hands on her hips, Mandy shook her head. "I can't believe you, Sable. I thought when you left here last night you were going to make up with Gage, not say good-bye to him! You bitch and complain that all men ever want from you is an easy lay, then you meet one who wants more, and you turn chicken."

That hurt. Sable knew she should never have told Miranda that Gage said he loved her. While it was obvious from the change in Mandy's vocabulary that she was getting more and more comfortable in the pub, she still came from a different world than Sable and would never understand why sometimes love didn't conquer all. Of course, maybe if she told Mandy that she'd seen Gage holding hands with another women less than a week after he'd confessed his love, she'd understand.

"I am not chicken," she muttered through gritted teeth as she continued to tear lettuce for the salads. "I'm realistic. Gage has moved on, and I should too."

Silence.

Sable glanced at Miranda, saw her rolling her eyes at Jake, and lost it.

"Look, Miranda, we've had this discussion before. Not all of us believe in happily ever after. But just because I don't believe in it doesn't mean I don't care about Gage. I don't want to see him hurt, and we're too different. Nothing will come of us trying to take things further than they've already gone, but hurt. We're just too different."

"He loves you," Miranda cried, exasperated. "Why can't you accept it? Why can't you let yourself believe that you could have it all?"

Ignoring the flare of hope in her heart, Sable continued to tear the lettuce, her movements getting more frantic as she talked. "He's got a house and a career...I've got a backpack and a camera. He's got a family he's close to...I haven't talked to mine in over a year. He wants to settle here, and I have a job waiting for me in Toronto. How can you possibly think we could have it all?"

Miranda reached out and covered her hands. Tugging them, she turned Sable to face to her. "Remember how we met? We were nine years old, and you were playing football with your brother and his friends. I was sitting on the grass wishing I could play, but too scared to try something new. You came over and asked me to join your team, and when I said I didn't know how to play, that I didn't think I could ever play such a physical game, you just laughed. Do you remember what you said to me?"

Miranda's eyes hardened when Sable nodded silently. "You said, 'You can do anything if you really want to.' You need to decide if you want it all, Sable, because if you want it...all you have to do is take it."

Sable watched Mandy walk away and turned to Jake, who'd heard every word in the empty bar. He would understand why she was calling it quits with Gage. But when she looked at him, his expression was one of disappointment.

"What?" she snapped at him.

He just shook his head and started for the kitchen.

"What, Jake? You have no opinion on the subject?" Anger flashed through her uncontrollably. "You, of all people, should understand that some of us are just meant to be alone."

Jake stopped dead still at that comment and turned to her slowly. "You're right. I do understand that some people are meant to be alone, but you're not one of them. You're just using the job as an excuse to run away."

Uncertainty seeped into her soul. "What makes you say that?" she asked, trying to stay angry. Anger was safe; she knew how to deal with anger.

Jake looked into her eyes and Sable was shocked at the pain she saw there. "You're a lot like my wife was. She was so tough and confident on the outside, but on the inside, she was just a woman wanting to be loved for who she was, not how she looked."

Jake had been married? Did Miranda know?

He closed his eyes, as if he could still see her in his mind. "Gage is everything you've never let yourself believe in. He sees past your looks to the real you, and that scares you more than anything, because if things don't work out, you can't blame it on him being a typical, shallow male." He opened his eyes again, and Sable felt as if he could see into her soul. His gaze strayed from her to the office where Miranda had disappeared, his voice was so full of raw emotion when he spoke that her heart ached for whatever he hid in his past. "You and Gage have a chance at true happiness here, and I think you're an idiot not to grab it with both hands."

Chapter Eighteen

Gage stepped inside the Zodiac and searched for Sable.

Katie was at a table flirting with a group of college-age guys and Miranda was behind the bar. He scanned the room, but Sable was nowhere to be seen.

Where the hell was she?

Jake had said she wasn't due to leave until tomorrow, but what if she'd left a day early? What if he'd missed her? Not possible. He couldn't have missed her.

He'd thought that giving her a week to think about things before chasing after her was smart. Apparently, it wasn't.

When he got home from work, less than an hour ago, there was a message on his machine from Jake demanding he call him back, right away. They'd been playing phone tag for the past two days, but the urgency in Jake's voice had never been so clear until today.

Gage finally got hold of Jake and was told that Sable had quit her job and was leaving town. His heart had stopped...then started pounding double time.

He couldn't let her get away! She'd chased him relentlessly until he fell in love with her, and then she wanted to run away? Uh-uh, there was no way in hell he was letting her go. Not without a fight.

He made his way to the bar and perched on a stool a few feet from Jim, Bruce, and Pops. He wasn't there to see them and he didn't particularly want them listening in when he cornered Sable.

Miranda looked up from where she was counting money, and smiled at him. "Hey, stranger, I'll be right there."

He nodded and smiled in acknowledgment. His fingertips tapped out a staccato rhythm on the bar and he deliberately took a deep breath. He had to stay in control; he had to find out what was going on.

The door to the back office was closed. Maybe that's where she was?

"What can I get you to drink?" Miranda asked cheerfully.

"A coffee would be great." He strove to be civil. "How are you?"

"I'm doing all right." She reached for the nearby pot and poured him some coffee. She placed it, along with a bowl full of cream and sugar, in front of him.

"It's been pretty quiet." She gestured at the half empty bar. "Which makes it a great night for me to work the bar."

"Are you planning on working the night shift with Sable leaving?" And why was she here instead of Sable right now?

"Not forever, but until I find a replacement, yes."

He grunted something non-committal. *Did that mean Sable wasn't here?*

As if she could read his mind, her lips tilted sympathetically and she spoke softly. "She's in the kitchen, Gage. She should be right back."

He nodded and took a gulp of coffee, scalding his tongue. A strange calmness settled over him, and for the first time since he talked to Jake, he felt as if he could finally breathe. She was still here.

"What are you going to do?" she asked.

"What makes you think I'm going to do something? Maybe I'm just here to say good-bye?"

"I've known Sable a long time, and I know when she's happy. As much as she says this job is what she wants, I know she's lying. To me and to herself." She stared at him earnestly. "She's been quiet as a mouse ever since she walked in the door an hour ago, and now you're here, tense as a cat ready to pounce on said mouse. I think *something* is about to happen."

Just then Sable strolled around the corner and stepped behind the bar. He released a breath he hadn't been aware of holding. His chest ached at the sight of her and he felt renewed faith that things would work out between them. Nothing was impossible when you set your mind to it. That was his motto, and Sable's too. Now he just had to convince her to apply it to them.

"Go easy on her, Gage. Love and trust are new emotions to her." Miranda patted his arm and stepped back.

Sable spotted him talking with Miranda and sashayed over, flashing that naughty smile that made his cock twitch. As if nothing had ever happened between them.

Her tight black shirt was unbuttoned just enough to hint at her generous cleavage and tucked into a red and black plaid skirt that ended mid-thigh. A creamy expanse of bare leg was visible before shiny black boots covered her from knee to toe. Her hair bounced around her shoulders, reminding him of how she looked when she was naked and riding him.

"Hey, Sexy," she purred. "How are you doing tonight?"

Her walk and talk were all confident, sexy attitude, but when he gazed into her baby blues he thought he caught a glimpse of...longing?

His heart soared, and remembering Miranda's warning, he kept his tone light. "Much better now."

"Hard day?" She leaned a hip against the back-bar, and crossed her legs at the ankles. A casual pose she didn't quite pull off.

"Long day that turned bad when I got a certain phone call." He studied her, trying to decipher what she was thinking, but Miranda was right. Her walls were in place, and after that initial peek, her eyes were giving nothing away either.

"Things are pretty quiet, Sable," Miranda spoke up. "Why don't you go sit and have a drink with Gage? I can handle these guys." She waved her arm in the direction of the regulars, all totally engrossed in the swimsuit special on the big screen TV.

He watched Sable arch a delicate eyebrow at Miranda. "Are you sure?"

"No problem." She smiled at them both. "It's your last night in town, you don't need to be here at all."

Sable shot a sharp glance his way, a small frown marring her forehead.

"Don't worry," he said when their eyes met. "I already know about the job offer." *And I'm here to make you a better one.*

"Oh!" she said quietly. "Okay, well, do you want to shoot some pool with me, then?"

No, he didn't want to play pool. He wanted to sit down and talk. But he knew she wouldn't go for that. She was running scared, and talking was the last thing she was interested in.

So they headed over to the pool area and Gage racked the balls while she selected a cue. Wasting no time, she bent over and took the first shot, sending the colored orbs in all directions.

He watched as she walked around the table, eyes on the set up, focus on the game. The smooth skin of her upper thighs was visible when she bent over the table. His gut tightened and he fought to stay calm. She barely looked at him, and his grip tightened on the cue stick to keep from grabbing her and pulling her into the office. He knew she wouldn't be able to say no to a last fuck. But he wanted so much more than that from her, for them.

She missed a shot and waved him toward the table. He looked down. She'd sunk three of her balls, leaving him with an easy corner shot. He bent at the waist, lined up his shot, and missed.

He didn't even care that he missed. His mind was not on the game at all, but on what to do next with Sable.

She tried to joke around a bit while they continued to play, but she wasn't her regular self. She was flirting too hard, her smile not quite reaching her blank eyes.

When she lined up her final shot and sank the eight ball, she stood and smiled. "I guess we should've made a bet on that game, huh?"

A half-baked idea began to form, and he couldn't stop a grin from spreading across his face for the first time that day. "We can place bets on the next game."

He knew what he wanted to win from her. And he *would* win this game. *Motivation was the key.*

An answering grin spread across her luscious lips. "What do you want if you win?"

Spotting Katie nearby, he waved her over and took two cardboard coasters and a pen off her tray. Handing one of the coasters to Sable, he flipped his over and quickly wrote on the back of his.

He handed the pen to Sable. "Write down what you truly want. We'll reveal them when the game's over."

She searched his gaze, panic and excitement warring clearly in her own. For the first time since he'd walked in the door that day, he got a glimpse of the woman he knew. The woman he loved.

She was gorgeous, she was sexy, and she was all his. She just didn't know it yet.

Y Y Y Y

Sable's hand trembled when she handed the pen back to Katie. What was she doing? She looked down at the words she'd written.

A real relationship. Us. Together. Forever.

They seemed so foreign—she was asking for something she hadn't thought she'd want. Something she'd never let herself believe was possible for her.

She couldn't believe she would even consider turning down a photography job for a man, especially a man who was seeing another woman. But Jake had been right, Gage was everything she'd never let herself believe in. How could she *not* give it a chance?

Even if she did win the bet, there was no guarantee Gage would give her what she wanted. There was no guarantee he *could* give her what she wanted. But wasn't the chance at happiness better than nothing?

She watched as Gage slipped his coaster into his back pocket and went to rack the balls again. His smiling face seemed somehow at odds with his determined movements. She watched him...the sound of her own heartbeat filling her ears.

Dreams of love, family, and happily ever after washed over her. Dreams she hadn't let herself have for too many years.

Gage stepped back from the table and gestured at the cue ball. "Your move, milady," he said with a playful grin.

Her move? A shiver danced down her spine.

Trying not to read too much into his odd choice of words, she stepped up to the table and tried to focus.

With a snap of her wrist, the cue ball shot across the table and broke up the others. But not one went down.

Disappointment stabbed her in the heart, and she realized the game was no longer fun for her. She wanted what she'd written on that coaster. More than she wanted any job.

In order to get a chance at that, she needed to win.

Determination rose within her as she observed the man that had stolen her heart walk around the pool table. This time when he bent over the table to take his shot her gaze didn't linger on his tight ass, but on his face, the lips she wanted to kiss forever...the eyes that saw the real her...and the bad-boy grin she saw in her dreams.

The face she wanted to see every morning when she awoke. It didn't matter that he'd started dating another woman. He'd tried to resist her once before and she'd won him over. She could definitely do it again, only this time, it would be for everything.

He didn't even look at her when the first ball dropped into the corner pocket. He just continued around the table and lined up his next shot. Only after sinking the third, and missing the fourth, did he look up. With a small smile that didn't reach the shadows in his eyes, he gestured her to the table.

Gone was the playful banter they usually shared, a thick tension in its place. For a second, she didn't think she'd get another chance at winning, and she'd felt the possible loss deep in her chest.

Eyeing the pool table, she carefully planned her strategy. She focused and went after what she wanted.

And managed to sink two balls before missing the third by a millimeter.

Frustration roared through her veins at her failure. Stepping back, she closed her eyes and sucked in a deep breath. Blowing it out between pursed lips, she lifted her head to meet Gage's stare head on.

Sable looked into those coffee colored depths and decided right then and there. He was The One. He was the one that could give her what she wanted, if only she was brave enough to forget about playing games and tell him exactly what she was thinking.

Taking a deep breath that did nothing to ease the ache in her chest, she set the pool cue on the table and walked toward him.

"I'm done with games, Gage," she said softly. Reaching for the coaster she'd set aside, she held it out for him to read.

"I want it all. I want happily ever after, and the only way I'm going to get it is if you agree to stick with me. I know I suck at relationships, but I'm tired of running. I've always told myself I wasn't walking away from people when they tried to get inside my head or tried to understand me, and I was right. I didn't walk away. I ran. I still don't know how you did it, but not only did you get inside my head, you got inside my heart." She paused to catch her breath, quickly putting a finger against his lips when he tried to interrupt.

"I'm not done yet, and if you don't let me say it all now, I might never get up the courage to say this again."

She waited until his mouth closed. She saw love and pride lighting up his dark eyes, and with a surge of hope, plunged ahead. "You make me feel things I never thought I would. Things I didn't think I *could* feel. And it scares the crap out of me. I told myself not to confuse this thing between us for love...but I was wrong. When I woke up that morning in your arms and realized that I wanted to be there every morning, I panicked and ran. I don't care if you've got a new girlfriend because I'm going to do whatever it takes to prove to you that I'm the one for you. I don't want to run anymore, from you or from my feelings. I love you, Gage. And I want the happily ever after I never thought was possible for me until now."

She smiled at him tremulously, unaware of the tears streaming down her cheeks until she tasted them on her lips.

Without a word, he reached into his back pocket and pulled out his coaster. Sable's breath froze in her throat when he looked at his coaster before turning it over so she could see the words.

I love you. I want you to take a chance on me. On us!

With a laughing hiccup, she took the coaster from his fingers, tossed it onto the pool table, and leapt into his open arms.

Gage let out a loud whoop as she rained kisses on his stubbled jaw. "You bet I will!"

She grinned at him through her tears. His mouth settled firmly on hers, and she felt like she was home. When they pulled apart to catch their breath, she became aware of the laughter and clapping surrounding them.

She grinned wickedly at Gage.

"Finally, no more head-games for us...just sex games!"

Three months later

Sable pulled the mail from the newly installed mailbox before entering Gage's refinished house. The house they'd made into a home over the last few months. She was no longer restless. She almost felt settled, with no urge to leave her newfound family.

She set down the grocery bags she'd been carrying, and tossed the mail on the counter. They fanned out and a colorful postcard caught her eye.

It was from Prague.

She turned it over and read the brief note. With a shout of joy, she dashed out the patio door to where Gage's family, along with Jake, Miranda, and Katie were gathered for the last barbecue of the year before the snow fell. They were celebrating the success of Sable's first photo exhibit. Her sold-out exhibit at the Chester Showroom.

At her shout, all heads turned in her direction, and she searched for the face dearest to her.

"Gage!" she yelled.

She jogged across the lawn, waving the postcard in front of her. "It's from my brother! He's coming to visit, and he'll be here in time for the wedding!"

Sasha White

Romance with Heat, Erotica with heart.

Sassy women and sexy men are what Canadian author Sasha White's stories are all about. After fifteen years as a bartender, she's decided the stories in her head need to be put down for other people to enjoy as well. Gifted with a salacious imagination, Sasha has over a dozen erotic stories published in print or electronically, with many more to come.

She enjoys working in several genres such as contemporary, paranormal, suspense and science fiction. Along with her ebooks here at Samhain Publishing, Sasha also has several new erotica stories to be released in 2006 with Kensington APHRODISIA and Berkley HEAT. She loves to hear from readers and chat with everybody so drop by her website at http://www.sashawhite.net and leave a comment on her blog. She can be found there most afternoons.

Let's Pretend

© *2006 Raine Weaver*
Available now in electronic and print books!

The art of subtle seduction can be a light-hearted game-or a deadly dance.

Veronica Peale is playing a game.

Her best friend Kayla has decided to "loan" Ronnie her newest boy-toy, all in an effort to make her boss, Paul Lang, insanely jealous. Veronica reluctantly agrees to pretend that she's having a torrid love affair with Brant Coleman in order to entice the man she really wants.

At least, she thinks he's the man she really wants...

Brant Coleman is also playing a game. He is, in reality, an insurance investigator, trying to discover why Ronnie is in possession of a priceless pair of antique earrings, reported stolen by one of the wealthiest families in Cleveland, Ohio. It is his job to verify that they are the stolen earrings and, if possible, to recover them. And if he has to pretend to be Kayla's tool and Veronica's lover to get what he wants, so be it.

At least, he thinks he's pretending to be in love with her...

Here is an excerpt from this tantalizing contemporary treat—

Ronnie swung the door open with a crippling yawn, then gave her visitor a venomous stare. "Coleman? What are you doing here? What time is it?"

That irresistible smile blazed forth. "You look like Linus of the Charlie Brown series standing there with your blankee."

She pulled the fleece coverlet around herself. For the first time she was grateful that her taste in sleepwear didn't lean toward sheer and frilly, or anything like the slinky negligees Kayla always wore. She felt awkward and exposed enough in her brushed-cotton gown. "I'll bet you say that to all the big-headed kids. What do you want?"

He entered unbidden, walking straight past her into her kitchen and starting her coffeemaker. "I wanted to catch you before you left for work. Be sure we're on the same page, so to speak."

She sighed heavily, trying her best to be angry with him. It was difficult. He'd brought the fresh air and newness of the morning into her tiny kitchen, just by walking in the door. "Brant. I haven't showered. Haven't changed. Haven't had any caffeine, haven't even faced a mirror yet. I may look like Linus, but I feel like Pigpen. Give me a break."

He looked surprised, as if it had never occurred to him to notice how she looked. "Oh. Sorry. I was just so enthusiastic about our little game...go ahead and get ready for your day. I know how you are about your 'routine'. I'll entertain myself. Where's Kayla?"

Ronnie's eyes shot to every alternate corner of the room. Uh-oh. This could be sticky. She had no idea how close the two of them were.

She opted for honesty. "She...she stayed out all night. I don't know where she is. I hope that's not a problem."

"Why should it be? I can catch her later," he responded simply. "Here, buddy."

She reached for the small paper bag he held out to her. "What's this? I can't accept..."

"Oh, don't get your undies in a wedge about it. Do you wear undies under that thing?" He grabbed the hem of her gown and began to ease it up.

"Stop that." She slapped his hand, fighting off a nervous giggle as her body temperature soared dangerously high. "It's none of your business."

"Oh, but it is *now*, Ronnie-rum." He snared her fingers and pulled her to his side. "It might be important, if we can get Pang to take the bait."

She pulled her hand back, retreating. "You keep your nose out of my underwear, Coleman. What's in the bag?"

"Open it."

She obeyed and, frowning, immediately handed it back to him. "I don't use this stuff."

"What's the big deal? It's only lipstick and perfume."

No, it wasn't. It was proof that he didn't think she was attractive enough as she was. "I don't use much of this stuff, unless there's some special occasion. When I go to the office, I'm going to do a job, not to—" Her objection died on her lips. It wasn't true anymore, was it? She *did* have an ulterior motive—trying to attract Paul Lang.

"The perfume's generic. As for the lipstick—the dark red one's for drama. And the gloss is just a dusky-rose sort of tint. Sort of like your lips," he added casually, apparently not noticing the color come to her cheeks. "After all, the original purpose of lipstick was to attract the attention of the male by subtly mimicking the female's swollen, flushed labia during sexual stimulation."

She buried her face in her blanket. "Thanks, 'buddy'. That really makes me want to run into the bathroom and smear it right on."

"Why are you embarrassed? What's wrong with letting a man know you're sexually interested and available?"

Why was he always asking her questions she couldn't answer? "You seem to have made an intense study of human nature."

He shrugged, handing her half a cup of coffee. "When you know what motivates people, you know why they behave the way they do. And you know what pleases them. Helps in the escort business."

She fidgeted indecisively with the bag. It wouldn't hurt, she supposed, to add a little color and scent to her business attire. Especially if it ended this awkward conversation. "All right. I'll try it. But just a *little*. Wouldn't want to attract *too* much attention to my labia."

He spread his arms wide. "That's all I ask. Now get ready. I'll drive you."

"No." The man was taking over her *life*. "I prefer to drive myself."

"Okay. Then I'll bring a little something later, and we can have lunch together. Now, now, don't say no. How about a simple donut in a plain paper bag? What could be wrong with that?"

* * * *

She should have known better.

She should have known she couldn't trust him.

Brant strolled into her office promptly at twelve thirty, captivating the ladies with his smile. All work stopped at the sight of the navy-blue knit shirt stretched across the broad band of chest, and the showy red-and-gold bag he carried before him, the one he set triumphantly upon her desk for all to see.

It was the trademark bag of "The G-Spot", the boutique well-known in certain circles for selling intriguing little objects and clothing to enhance the sex life of eager couples. The name of the store was emblazoned across the bag; and the fact that the bag was so small made it seem even more intriguing.

She slowly massaged her forehead as he leaned across her desk, his voice deep with amusement. "Whassup, Ronnie-rum. Did you miss me?"

"Please tell me," she mumbled, her mouth hidden behind her hand, "that you have an *edible* donut in that bag."

"Two, in fact." He smirked. "Edible? Of course. What other kind would they be?"

"I was afraid they might be...you know, maybe the little round rubber rings you put around a...that men use for..."

"Yessss?" The smirk became a pudding smile.

Long Distance Love
Anne Whitfield
Now available in ebook!

Can one delicious summer affair be enough to keep them together?

Fleur Stanthorpe, an Australian, arrives in Whitby, England to live out a dream. She's to open a bookshop café and experience the English way of life for the summer before returning home and settling down.

Only she hasn't counted on meeting gorgeous Irishman, Patrick Donnelly. Their attraction is instant - their goals a world apart. He is looking for a solid relationship. She is having her last fling at freedom before returning home to family and responsibilities.

Their problems are more than surviving a hot summer of romance, but wondering what will happen when the summer draws to an end and Fleur returns to the other side of the world.

Looking for love in far off places? Check out this steamy excerpt from Long Distance Love.

Deciding to head for the car, Fleur saw Patrick emerge from behind a stall, licking a large ice cream; in his other hand he held one for her.

As she drew near, she grinned and raised her eyebrows. "Where have you been? I thought you were coming straight back?"

He licked his ice cream and winked. "I got sidetracked. I had other things on my mind."

"Like ice cream?" She gave him a saucy look, but her insides melted whenever he smiled at her. Together they turned for the car.

He held out her cone. "Ice cream is very important. You simply can't go out for the day and not have one. It's tradition."

She laughed and held up the bags. "How can I eat it with this lot?"

"Oh dear. Looks like I'll have to eat yours too then." He laughed, but just then a large raindrop splattered onto his ice cream and he frowned in surprise, which made Fleur giggle.

The rain fell heavier, and a clap of thunder rolled in the distance. People started to move quicker, heading for their cars as the only shelter, while the sellers hurriedly packed up their goods.

"I think we'd better run for it," Patrick said, squinting into the windblown rain.

They ran through the rows of cars looking for Patrick's navy BMW. On a hasty mission to get into the car without getting any more soaked than they already were, Patrick, juggling ice creams in one hand, opened the boot for Fleur to throw in the bags on top of the others. Hurrying, they jumped into the car and slammed the doors.

Fleur glanced at Patrick, dripping not only rain from his hair but also ice cream from the cones he held in each hand, and laughed. Despite his appearance she thought he looked damn fine. Sexy as hell.

A box of Kleenex sat between the seats and she grabbed a couple and went to wipe the dripping, sticky mess.

"Can you wipe my eyes first?" He chuckled. "I can't see properly."

Leaning over, she gently wiped his wet face. Her movements were long and leisurely. She liked having the opportunity to touch him in all innocence. Yet, when she caught his gaze, his eyes were dark with unspoken messages and the pit of her stomach curled in anticipation. Innocent, her backside. Wicked thoughts plagued her.

Slowly he bent forward and touched his lips to hers. Her breathing seemed suspended between her lungs and throat. Her hand holding the Kleenex fell to his shoulder as she leaned in closer, wanting so much more than he was giving her at the moment.

Their kiss deepened, intensified. His tongue stroked hers in a slow dance, tasting, exploring. An ache spread from the very core of her to reach from the top of her head to her toes. Heat flamed her body.

"I've wanted to kiss you since the first day I saw you," he murmured.

"Me too..." She leaned back a little and smiled shyly.

"I haven't fancied anyone for a long time, you know that?" Patrick leaned forward and kissed her nose and then her eyes. "Then you came along and the instant I saw you I was lost for words."

"Really?" Wide-eyed she stared at him. "It didn't seem that way."

A wry smile lifted the corners of his mouth. "Do you think I just invite anyone for a free meal at my restaurant? I had to get to know you."

"I'm so glad you did."

"Mmm... I am too."

She pressed herself against his chest. That he still held the cones and couldn't touch her with anything but his mouth made it so erotic.

As if reading her mind, he brought his cone in between them.

Together they licked the melting ice cream and then kissed, sometimes transferring the confectionary into each other's mouths. Fleur used her finger to dip into the ice cream and then traced around his lips with it. The tip of her tongue followed the pattern she made and Patrick groaned deep in his chest.

In seconds he had opened the door, thrown both cones out and slammed the door shut again.

As the rain beat hard against the windscreen, he dragged her over the seat divide and onto his lap. Holding her tight, he kissed her with mounting passion until she could barely breathe. He created a blaze of fire within her and she felt she would self-combust if he didn't quench the ache soon.

Samhain Publishing, Ltd.

It's all about the story...

Action/Adventure
Fantasy
Historical
Horror
Mainstream
Mystery/Suspense
Non-Fiction
Paranormal
Red Hots!
Romance
Science Fiction
Western
Young Adult

http://www.samhainpublishing.com